A Selection from Dino Buzzati

The
SIREN

Chosen and Translated by Lawrence Venuti

North Point Press · *San Francisco* · *1984*

These translations are published by arrangement with Arnoldo Mondadori Editore, S.p.A., Milano. *Barnabo della montagne* (Barnabo of the Mountains) © 1933 by Arnoldo Mondadori Editore; *Il borghese stregato* (The Bewitched Bourgeois), *Scorta Personale* (Personal Escort), and *Storia interrotta* (An Interrupted Story) were published in *Paura alla Scala* (© 1948 by Arnoldo Mondadori Editore); *Un verme in casa* (The Gnawing Worm), *La macchina che fermava il tempo* (The Time Machine), and *I cinque fratelli* (The Five Brothers) were published in *Il crollo della Baliverna* (© 1954 by Arnoldo Mondadori Editore); *Il tappeto volante* (The Flying Carpet) and the epigraph to this volume (*Il Califfo ci aspetta*) were published in *In quel preciso momento* (© 1955 by Arnoldo Mondadori Editore); *La parola proibita* (The Prohibited Word) and *La peste motoria* (The Plague) were published in *Sessanti racconti* (© 1958 by Arnoldo Mondadori Editore; *Riservatissima al signor direttore* (Confidential) was published in *Il colombre* (© 1966 by Arnoldo Mondadori Editore); *Racconto a due* (Duelling Stories) and *Una serata difficile* (A Difficult Evening) were published in *Le notti difficili* (© 1971 by Arnoldo Mondadori Editore). *Le case di Kafka* (Kafka's Houses) appeared in the *Corriere della Serra* of 31 March 1965.

Grateful acknowledgment is made to the National Endowment for the Arts for a grant that supported the work on this translation.

For Angelo and Philomena Sabato

Contents

Preface

When North Point Press expressed interest in publishing a second volume of Dino Buzzati's fiction, I did not hesitate to accept their invitation to edit and translate it. Buzzati is a writer to whom I was already deeply committed, and I was delighted with this opportunity to make more of his writing available to an English-language audience. Despite my enthusiasm, however, I still had to solve the crucial problem faced by every editor of a "selected works": On what basis would texts be included or omitted? It turned out that Buzzati himself was to provide the criterion I was seeking.

At the start of the project, as I was reading through his hundreds of stories and sketches, I recalled an entry in his notebooks. "Every writer and artist," he wrote, "however long he may live, says only one thing. . . . There are renowned painters who for their entire lives paint the same identical landscape, the same still life, the same figures." He added that this state of affairs is "inevitable. Otherwise they would not be sincere. Besides, does not the style by which a writer's personality is distinguished perhaps imply a certain uniformity or, better yet, a certain identity of meaning?"

The more I read in Buzzati's work, the more I realized that these remarks have a special application to him, and I finally decided to use them as the criterion of my selection. They fascinated not because they licensed a search for Buzzati's "personality" (always a risky enterprise), but because they insisted on a sameness in the face of obvious differences, an identity that transcended—and in a way denied—the vicissitudes of a prolific career that spanned over four decades. And so I planned an unusual retrospective of Buzzati's fiction: it would begin with his first published work, the novella *Barnabo of the Mountains*, and reveal a developing preoccupation with recurrent landscapes, characters, motifs, structures.

This decision transformed the entire process of producing the book, infusing it with that air of suspense and discovery that Buzzati so skillfully cultivates in his writing. As I chose and translated the stories, his distinctive preoccupations emerged in striking, even uncanny ways. The resemblances proliferated, although always qualified with a provocative difference that enriched them and avoided mere repetition. I found that while the stories were quite effective on their own, they could also be read as penetrating commentaries on one another. In the end, the manuscript reverberated with unexpected meanings and acquired an internal coherence that belies the very notion of a selected works.

The stories are drawn from most of the collections that were published during Buzzati's lifetime, and I have added one of his newspaper articles, "Kafka's Houses," a characteristic travel essay that first appeared in *Corriere della Sera*. The result, it seems to me, is a varied sampling of Buzzati's writing that can claim to be not only representative, but informed by the "identity of meaning" that he mentions in his notebook entry. Whether this strategy has allowed me to include his best efforts, I leave to the reader to decide.

L. V.

In the squalid boarding houses of the old quarters, in the bare tenements on the outskirts, someone suddenly gets out of bed, in the dead of night, runs into the hallway, and wakes the other tenants. "Let's set off!" he shouts, inflamed by incomprehensible hopes. His face has become radiant. Is it a miracle? No one complains about being wakened at that absurd hour. "Where are we heading?" a woman asks with a smile, looking out from the door of her room. "The Americas," someone proposes with enthusiasm. "The Indies!" "Pannonia," says another voice. "The Caliph awaits us!" Oblivious to the difficulties, they excitedly discuss the journey, an inexplicable haste has seized them, they feel lighthearted, and the injustice of those wretched walls, those torn robes, those foul odors, those flaccid faces, all that bitter truth is denied in the poetry of the night. "Come on, hurry!" he urges. "The bags! The cloaks! The ship is about to sail. Don't you hear the siren?"

Dino Buzzati

The
SIREN

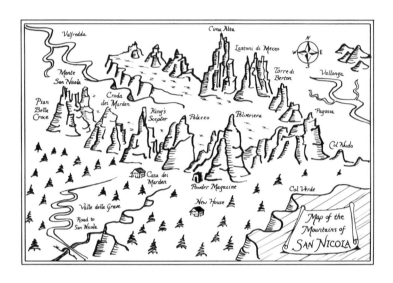

Map of the Mountains of SAN NICOLA

Barnabo of the Mountains

I

No one remembers when the house was built for the foresters from the village of San Nicola. Also known as Casa dei Marden, it was located in Valle delle Grave, at the foot of the mountains. Five paths emanated from that point and entered the forest. One descended into the valley toward San Nicola, gradually turning into a true road. The other four rose amid the trees, becoming increasingly uncertain and narrow, until nothing remained of the forest but dry, uprooted trunks and all its ancient legends. Above, to the north, was the white gravel that shrouds the mountains.

The sun rises from the great peaks, turns over Casa dei Marden, and sets behind Col Verde. The wind blows at nightfall, carrying away another day. Del Colle, the commander of the foresters, is in rare form today and has long stories to tell. Only he remembers them, but if he tried to tell them all, it would take a night and the following morning and they still would not be finished.

There is the story of Ermeda, the rich gentleman of San Nicola: "He was coming from Vallonga with his three men. When they neared Col Nudo, the fog started to settle. He took the wrong path, went down into a gorge and came out on a broad ledge beneath the Pagossa. At this point he couldn't see anymore; he would have to wait until tomorrow, when the sun would show him the way back. But he was never found, and they say that they spent months searching for him under the cliffs. That was many years ago."

There is the story of the powder magazine. They planned to build a road that would join San Nicola to Vallonga. The authorities had an agreement. Old Bettoni took on the project. The road was to climb the slope of Valle delle Grave, then turn left, skirting the Palazzo, running parallel to the chain of the Pagossa and finally passing beyond Col Nudo. The work began at San Nicola. It was a momentous undertaking. The workers arrived from the lowlands. They had to blast the mountain. They bought enormous quantities of powder and deposited them in a small shed at the base of the Palazzo.

But at the end of the first ravine, when the workers had to set off some of the charges, construction was brought to a standstill. The powder didn't explode; at night tools were stolen. Down in the village it was rumored that the thing was insane—money thrown away. Over and over people said that the mountains must remain tranquil. And the bells of San Nicola were rung so that the evil spirits might leave.

One night a worker went to rob a house. Afterward Bettoni was blamed because he didn't supervise his workers adequately. His rival, who lost the contract for the road, fed the fire. There were threats to blow up the shed where the explosives were stored.

It was then that in the side of one mountain, just above the point where the road was to pass, they found a sort of grotto, filled it with the powder, sealed it off behind a wall, and stationed the foresters there to do guard duty. Meanwhile, the construction stopped for the winter, and the year after, when the workers returned, it was discovered that the project was short of money. Today there remains a brief stretch of road that reaches only as far as the Palazzo; farther on, the path that leads to the Polveriera continues.

One day some military officers passed by on patrol and saw the powder magazine: it is beautifully constructed and stands in a well-sheltered place, not far from the border. Therefore it must be utilized. Some ammunition and more explosives were brought there, but the foresters remained in their role as guard. Things went unchanged for years. Even now before the door that opens into the living rock a man paces back and forth with a rifle. Every night his relief, a detail of three men, sets out from Casa dei Marden and walks for two hours through the woods, arriving at the magazine near the small shed.

And then there is the story of Darrìo. He too was a forester. "There are thieves in the mountains," he kept saying. "They escaped from prison and are hiding up there. One day or another they will come down to rob and destroy. We need to go and look for them." He left in the morning, walking straight through the forest and up the steep, stony slope of the mountainside. God only knows how he managed to scale the sheer rock walls. There are thieves, he said, but perhaps he didn't believe it. He spent entire days far away, on the edge of precipices. And yet brave as he was, he never came back. We waited and then searched the forest, pushing on as far as the gravel, our horns filling the mountains with echoes. And a week later did not Berton, as he was coming down from the magazine, see twelve or thirteen ravens whirling round and round over a very high wall? Darrìo had reached a peak just below the King's Scepter. His bones are still there, on a small terrace. In the end, he wanted to die.

Twelve foresters wearing green hats, in each of which a little feather has been inserted. Pinned to their jackets is a badge representing the village's coat of arms. The commander, Antonio Del Colle, with his white moustache, is already an old man, but he still climbs the mountains well and carries heavy loads. And when he shoots his rifle, no one has ever seen him miss. His English shotgun is always tucked in a leather case. Engraved on the barrel is a snake biting its tail. As a rule, Del Colle uses another weapon, a rifle he found in his house and doesn't have so much regard for. He is a short man. You can easily recognize him from a distance by his swaying step. He stops every so often to look around. He is old, this native of the mountains; he notices the diseases that infect the fir trees, knows the song of every bird, remembers all the narrowest paths. He feels the bad weather approaching. And he knows his men well: Giovanni Marden, who is second in command, and his cousin Paolo, Giovanni Berton, Pietro

Molo, Francesco Franze, Berto Durante, Angelo Montani, Primo and Battista Fornioi, Giuseppe Collinet, Enrico Pieri and Barnabo, whom they call only by his first name and who will henceforth be Barnabo of the Mountains.

It isn't easy to say where they came from. Some are the sons of foresters. Some were born into those patriarchal families in the mountains. Others have come from far away and have known the roads of the plain. But by now they have forgotten those infinite, dusty roads scorched by the sun. There was neither shade nor wind, and streams were rare. You could only keep going straight ahead. There, at the foot of the path, is a shady tree—one more effort. Your feet fall like lead, but don't lose heart! You have arrived.

2

The house that once belonged to the Marden family and now shelters the foresters has aged. The wooden beams are rotted and the shutters no longer close. One night Durante awoke because he felt cold. He got out of bed and lit a lamp. The wind had torn away a piece of the roof, just like that, silently.

Once the house was as bright and shiny as a newlyweds' cottage. There were flowers in windowboxes and everything was painted in different colors.

Now the plaster on the first floor has crumbled away, and the boards that panelled the second have turned black. The roof has gradually grown weary of counting the raindrops and debating with the wind; there are gaping holes, some shingles flew away, but nobody noticed it. The house is on the verge of collapsing; the slightest impact would smash it to pieces.

"Fornioi, the carpenter, fix the beams in the roof," said Del Colle. "At night they creak and they'll wind up splitting."

"But everything will be fixed tomorrow," thought Del Colle. "Tomorrow the sun will be propitious and there will be a desire to work. And yet time is passing today, not tomorrow, when it won't have passed yet." So, under their eyes, almost without their notice, Casa dei Marden deteriorated. Later on, when Durante realized that a piece of the roof had disappeared, the discussion began.

"We need to move now," he said to himself. "We're too far from the powder magazine. It's too humid here in the middle of the forest. Anyhow this house has to be rebuilt from scratch."

Del Colle was displeased. The kitchen was blackened from smoke and the odors of many meals had seeped into the walls. "It's a shame," he thought. "I have been living here for more than twenty years. I remember the first day I came. It was in the summer and it was raining. There isn't much to say. I spent my entire life in this house. Now, when I'm inside and I see the shotgun hanging on the bedpost, I forget about wanting a lot of money or staying in the village. What nonsense. I also suffered in this house and at certain times, many years ago, I had a desperate desire to go down to the plain. There was also someone who ran away. But I remember that he sang to himself in the fall, when Ermeda used to have the big hunt. I remember phenomenal meals, and old Da Rin trying to play the violin. There were winters, then summer came, then it was winter again. . . . I am old and now I must leave."

Del Colle also remembered that a few months after Darrìo's death he was urgently summoned to San Nicola. He arrived at nightfall, after a day overcast with gray clouds. With the inspector, who has authority over all the foresters in the province, he found a thin woman in tears, holding a rosary, and a short, disquieting gentleman. They were Darrìo's parents. They wanted their son's body at any cost. There was no persuading them that they were asking for the impossible. The father absolutely wanted to see—with his own eyes—the place where the corpse was found.

The mother remained at San Nicola. The father and Del Colle set out at dawn, without saying a word. The old man did not have climbing boots and yet he strode on furiously, his eyes fixed on the ground. All night it rained and the grass and plants were running with water. The mountains were still black beneath a curtain of clouds. They passed through the valley, then the forest, and went straight ahead without stopping.

"I want to go up as far as possible," said the old man and Del Colle led him over the gravel to the point where the walls rose. Around four hundred meters above, on a narrow ledge, Darrìo's bones lay scattered here and there, completely misshapen.

But the two men pushed farther on, laboriously climbing through the boulders in a tight ravine that ran behind a towering pyramid. Finally they stopped where the ravine was blocked off and jagged peaks rose straight up all around. A jet of rainwater gushed down through a black crevice. It was a dark, slimy cavern in the inaccessible wall. Hanging much higher were Darrìo's remains; they too had been drenched by the rain and were slowly drying. The old man stared at the rocks as if he were bewitched. The waterfall roared, and clouds passed slowly overhead.

"Do you want to return, sir? Do you see how impossible it is?" But the other didn't answer; he stared at the crags that overlapped in the sky. Del Colle looked at his watch: one hour, an hour and a half, two hours, they had to go down; the rain was about to start again. Darrìo's father moved only when the forester took him by an arm (the nocturnal shadows were falling) and said that it was late. The old man looked up once again. Then he started the descent, without saying a word.

3

They built the foresters' new house on the slope of the valley opposite Casa dei Marden. The structure is nearly the same, but the materials are entirely new, and the roof is made of zinc. The beautiful thing about the new house is that it is much farther up, very close to the powder magazine, in a large field surrounded by the forest. This is the inauguration day.

Many people arrive by the road that was purposely constructed for the house (it can also serve as a mule trail). It is a radiant Sunday in July. The men are wearing their best clothing, the women multicolored dresses. The foresters have also trimmed their beards and they are showing off their new uniforms. Del Colle is outside, on a most comfortable bench, talking about the time when Ermeda was still there and how he used to make the band play. "Then he died in the mountains and the musicians drifted away. Now no one knows how to play anymore. The old drum is down in the river; they threw it in the stream below the market square. Some of the iron parts are still there, all rusted."

It is noon in the tranquil clearing. Every so often the forest murmurs, and you can see all the lofty peaks very clearly. Today they are white, and luminous clouds cast shadows here and there: the three peaks of Monte San Nicola, the Croda dei Marden, the King's Scepter, then farther right, moving from west to east on the same ridge, the Palazzo, the Polveriera, and at the end, the outline of the Pagossa. Towering above them all and streaked with snow stand the Cima Alta and the Lastoni di Mezzo, which looks like four very thin campaniles.

Meanwhile the celebration begins. Two men who worked on the road begin playing dance music on harmonicas. Everyone is here, even the mayor and the inspector, both of whom are laughing. There is a great desire for entertainment in the air. In fact, a kind of new life is beginning. .

How splendidly Molo dances, whirling the mayor's daughter in his arms. Now Berton also steps forward and one-two-three, one-two-three, he too knows how to waltz, and perhaps better than the others. But why does the young Barnabo stand in the background? In the end he too takes a partner along with the others. Just then, however, the two harmonicas break off.

Del Colle now wants them to listen to some old music, those melodies from the past that conjure up his youth. He too has gone to get a harmonica. The tranquillity of the afternoon, the banners waving in the sun—the party has scarcely begun, it will go all night.

Del Colle plays the harmonica and the others listen quietly. Giovanni Marden stands near him; he smiles, watching Del Colle's fingers pressing the keys, hardly moving and yet making such delightful music. The banners have stopped waving. The wind has subsided so that everything is quiet when the old songs are played.

Bravo Del Colle! He is such a sprightly man. Yes, he is fifty-six years old, but listen to him play; and when he shoots his rifle, he doesn't miss a bottle at a hundred meters. "Hurray!" everyone shouts. The sun has turned slightly toward the west, but no one has noticed it. There is now talk of going down to the village. The mayor and the inspector have promised to buy drinks for everyone. A few people start down the road, laughing. The others catch up and they all walk together. Why isn't Del Colle coming? "Go on ahead," he answers. "I'll come at once. I've forgotten some papers at Casa dei Marden. I'm going to get them before I head for San Nicola."

"You can always get the papers tomorrow. Come with us now."

"What does an hour matter? I'll be there, you can bet on it. Our party is marvelous."

Everyone else has left. A great silence remains. Little by little the wind picks up again, making noises in the forest. "Coo . . . coo . . .

coo . . . coo." You can hear it from a distance. Del Colle will now go to Casa dei Marden. It is a downhill journey that will not take more than an hour. He has closed the green door, with its fresh coat of paint. After looking around, he begins to shuffle away. He reaches the foot of the clearing and gradually disappears. The new house is completely alone.

The sun grows fainter in the midst of the fir and larch trees and in a little while it will set behind Col Verde. The mountains have also changed with the passage of time. Many years ago you could find little spirits in the woods. Del Colle had seen them many times. They were so nimble and green as the fields. Could they have hindered the work on the road? It seems likely that with the occasional gunshots, the arrival of the workers, and the blasts from the construction, the spirits of the forest had been disturbed and who knows where they were hiding now.

He arrives before the old house as the forest is darkening, especially where the branches are dense. He pulls his harmonica from his pocket. Once it was just like this. The spirits used to love those songs and after a while, if night had already fallen, they appeared among the trees.

He plays and plays and in the meantime the sun sets. There is a soft noise, a branch snapping and falling, then crashing into the delicate leaves heaped on the ground. He hears another noise. Were the green-faced spirits returning, softly, softly, never harming a living soul? Del Colle notices that everything is like those times in his youth. There is Casa dei Marden, which could seem new in the darkness, with the tranquil forest and the fragrance of the evening. Yet Del Colle didn't have a beard then, nor were his veins so thick, his breathing so heavy. He recalls that he used to wear beautiful needlework on his jacket, and like the others, he had fallen in love, down at the dairy in San Nicola. On holidays they used to travel around the village all night, happily singing together.

A breeze blows through the treetops, and a very soft whisper erupts all around the small clearing. Have the spirits disappeared? Have they been frightened again? There is now a heavy silence, such as Del Colle has never heard in the woods. Straining his ears, he listens to steps approaching and makes out some human voices. It would be better to stay quiet; hide yourself behind a tree. In the dense shadows, the forester sees two men armed with rifles emerge from the woods. They are talking, but he can't hear what they are saying. One of them goes up to the house and tries to open the door. Here they are, then, those scoundrels.

Since the door is locked, the stranger starts to force it open. "Now I'll fix you," thinks Del Colle, whose heart has begun to pound. He leaps out from his hiding place and strides silently across the grass. One of the men sees him now and takes off toward the right, shouting to his companion: "Look out behind you!" But Del Colle has already seized the other by the shoulder, thrown him to the ground and grabbed his neck. "Now, you thief, you're coming with me!" he says, panting, and holds the man prisoner.

A gunshot rings out. There was a spurt of flame in the trees; the noise fades away, leaving the odor of gunpowder. Del Colle is wounded in a shoulder and falls. Blood gurgles in his throat. The thief, feeling the grip go slack, leaps to his feet and vanishes into the forest. Del Colle does not even shout: no one could hear him. He has a terrible pain in his shoulder; stretched out on the moist grass, his eyes open, he hears the blood gushing in his neck.

The murderers have fled. Del Colle notices that the forest has started to whisper again, and the tranquil breathing of the wind fills the vast silence. Far away, down in the village, his friends dance in the glare of huge torches; they have forgotten about Del Colle. Besides, he was old: he would be better off with the old ones, with the trees and the mountains. Yet now they have betrayed him, and his blood has bathed the earth.

4

The search goes on: Del Colle must be found. He said that he was going to Casa dei Marden. They found him in the morning, lying in the field in front of the house, already illuminated by the sun. Barnabo was the first to arrive, and he noticed that the commander was dead even before he was near him. Del Colle had to die this way, along with his house and his endless stories. Barnabo liked seeing the damaged roof and blackened boards of the old dwelling, those traces of its very long life, and nearby, stretched out on the grass, lay his commander, as the sun filtered through the branches. It was then that he was astonished at not feeling any grief. And yet his commanding officer was dead, a good man who loved everyone.

The night before, Del Colle had perhaps fallen asleep thinking of all the things that had happened in his life, all the men who had crossed that threshold. He lay there, absorbed in his imagination, and in the meantime his life was ending. This was really the best way, yet the others could not understand.

"He's dead!" shouted Barnabo when he heard the steps approaching. It was Giovanni Marden, followed by the other men. They all stood around the corpse, not daring to touch it. Then they saw a black stain on the grass. His jacket too was all dirtied with blood.

Perhaps a gust of wind blew over the high rocks; perhaps the water roared at the foot of the valley and some men were singing at the edge of the woods. Yet there, in the clearing, an oppressive silence hung in the air. The good Del Colle had been killed. The eyes instinctively turned to scrutinize the mountains, the clouds, the infinite trees, the house. But what could have changed?

"One night, a few months ago," says Giovanni Marden, "when they were starting to talk about the new house, a night when all of you were away, Del Colle spoke to me about his death. 'I don't have to worry about my daughter,' he said. 'She made a good marriage. As for me, I'm now at the end of the road. When I die, if it isn't too much trouble, you must bury me in a certain place.' And he told the story about Darrìo's father and described that ravine where they had stopped. 'Right at the base of a huge tower,' he told me, 'in the wall, to the right, there is a hole. When I saw it, I thought: here's your spot, Del Colle; this is where you can rest in peace.' And now, my friends," continues Marden, "we shall make him a coffin—you will make it, Fornioi—and then we will carry him up there. It will be an hour's walk."

The coffin is hammered together; it came out rather small, however, and the corpse's shoulders were cramped. The foresters lifted the box and carried it up over the gravel on a day when some gray clouds drifted far above the mountains. Is somebody watching them? Somebody, unseen, at the edge of the forest, who is afraid of letting himself be noticed? Yet now no one can observe them; the foresters have entered a steep ravine, inaccessible and solitary. The rocks roll down with a roar, but no one opens his mouth to speak. The coffin has grown heavy. A few meters more and the job will be over. They found the hole in the side of the mountain, to the right; the entire coffin fit inside easily. A huge rock was put over the opening.

Barnabo noticed that Berton suddenly walked away, but he didn't dare break the silence to call him. Climbing up a slanted ledge, Berton turned his back to them and inched up the wall of the tower that seals off the ravine. After a little while, they all saw him clinging to the vertical crags beneath the last stretch of sheer rockface. If he were not careful, there would be another disaster. While his colleagues looked at one another, Berton reached the slender peak. He was carrying Del Colle's old beret and he fastened it at the highest point with a nail. The body lies buried at the foot of the tower; at the top is the hat, with its distinctive feather. It is a beautiful grave.

5

Del Colle's story has made the rounds through all the valleys. "There are bandits in the mountains," people are saying. "Why wait to hunt them down and imprison them?" There is talk that the forester's murderers came from the border that lies behind the Cima Alta; it is thought that they were smugglers, used to robbing houses. The roads are deserted in the evening, and the other night a shadow was seen in San Nicola, near the church. Someone then took his gun from the wall, wiped it off and bought cartridges. A long stain remains where the rifle hung. And yet it seems like yesterday was the last time he used it. But you had only to see the rust inside the barrel. It seems like yesterday, and yet the stain slowly formed on the wall. This is precisely how time passes.

"Everyone is quick to say 'Search for them.'" The inspector is holding forth in San Nicola one night, sitting with a few of the villagers in the café on the square. "It would take months to go through the entire forest, and then who would risk climbing the peaks where there aren't even any trails?"

The others are silent, illuminated by the weak electric light. Outside, on the sidewalk, they hear steps every so often. A door slams inside the house. The clock ticks. They notice that every night is the same: always in the café, always those faces, those very words.

The square is badly lit by eight streetlamps and the houses all around are dark. No lights are burning in the deserted streets. But the wind is awake above, in the treetops, and someone is pacing, one–two, one–two, at the foot of the Polveriera throughout the night. Perhaps the moon is also rising, and the sentry becomes more alert, so much so that he thought he saw something moving near that huge rock. Meanwhile the moonlight strikes the foresters' new house and shines on the clearing, the grass, each of the stony paths. But no one sees all this light except for the sentry, whose heart (he hears it distinctly in the night) beats loudly.

The powder magazine stands at the mouth of a gorge between the Palazzo and the Polveriera, on a rocky spur that juts out into the gravel from the wall on the right. The cliffs loom overhead, hundreds and hundreds of meters away. Every so often, in the dead of night, something collapses and the sound roars in the ravines.

"Berton," says Barnabo in the guard's shed, calling his friend in the next bunk. The moonlight pierces the window, shining on a part of the floor. "Did you hear that noise?"

"Are you awake too? It must have been a landslide. I don't think those men are capable of scaling the walls. Especially not at night."

Silence. Outside they can hear the sentry pacing back and forth. Molo is on duty.

"Say," continues Berton, "you know what I'd like to go and see someday? What's behind that crest."

"Forget it," answers Barnabo. "It would be impossible: what has gotten into you? . . . Wait a minute."

Nothing is there. They hear only Molo's paces.

"Why? Did you hear something?"

"No, nothing. I just thought I did."

6

There was nothing but rain. For three days they had to stay shut up in the new house. Who would travel through the cold, dripping trees and the drenched fields? The mountains are constantly wrapped in whitish clouds.

Night arrives without anyone noticing it. The foresters have all gathered in the clearing. There are rifles to be oiled, many things to be put in place. One of them starts reading a book and, over there, in that dark corner, you can hear another softly singing to himself.

"Light the lamp, Collinet," says Giovanni Marden. It has grown so dark that they can't see one another.

Collinet lights the oil lamp, and the forest outside seems even darker.

"No news yet from the Polveriera?" asks Pietro Fornioi.

"Someone should have come down by now."

Who in fact has come? They hear knocking at the door.

Nothing unusual. It is Molo, arriving from San Nicola with the supplies, completely soaked from the rain.

"What brutal weather," he says. "Down the road, near the bridge, a ledge collapsed. If I hadn't gotten by quick enough, I would've been buried. I saw the inspector and the other regulars at the café, still talking about Del Colle. And I told them what they have to do."

"Just you, imagine."

"Just me. They said that I was perfectly right, and something will be done. Tomorrow morning a search party will set out for Vallonga, and another will head toward Pian della Croce."

"What are they going to do? What do they plan to search in the woods?" asks Marden.

"The dairies. They're hiding in the empty cottages. The question, it seems to me, is that nobody wants to do it. Del Colle is killed, and you just sit here around the fire."

"But why search the woods?" Barnabo asks then. "They went into the mountains. Isn't the real problem all the effort it takes to get up there?"

"And that's where you'd like us to go, is that right?" asks Molo with a sneer.

"I certainly won't be the one to say it."

"Darrìo wasn't good enough and you want to go? And how do you—"

"There are two trails through the mountains," the elder Fornioi brother interrupts. "One goes up, the other down. We'll take both. And then we'll write: Dear Inspector, Sir, we felt called upon to—"

"Cut it out, dammit!" shouts Marden. The others laugh. "Tomorrow morning Molo and Durante will go to Col Nudo and search as far as the dairies in Vallgona. Angelo and Primo Fornioi will take the other side, toward Pian della Croce."

"And you, Barnabo, climb the Cima Alta and lay in a supply of rocks," says Molo, walking over to the seated Barnabo and slapping him on the back.

Barnabo turns toward him enraged and seizes his arm.

"I wouldn't mind the effort, my friend, you don't know me."

Molo reddens and Barnabo stands in front of him, while the others shout: "Let's go, forget about it! Always arguing!"

But Molo has grabbed Barnabo around the waist; he is stronger and the grip hurts. "Del Colle played the harmonica, and everyone was there to see him," thinks Barnabo, as he manages to get his colleague's neck in a tightening armlock. "You're stronger, but now I'll send you on your ass."

Molo is stronger and yet he is about to submit; you can clearly see how he clenches his teeth in pain. This spectacle could be only a great embarrassment for him. As everyone watches, Barnabo notices that his adversary is suffering; he pretends to slip, loosens his hold and jumps backward. Molo straightens up again, panting, a stern expression on his face. "I said you couldn't take it, didn't I?" Barnabo has already gone out the door; he stands by the small porch at the entrance. It is still dripping in the darkness. From the house come the light, some loud voices, and a burst of hearty laughter.

There are noises in the house early next morning. Will the weather be good? They can't see yet; the thick fog that had blanketed everything is only now beginning to lift.

Molo, Durante, Montani, and Fornioi are about to depart. The others are still resting in their warm beds, listening to the noises and voices down in the kitchen. They are making coffee. They bustle about slightly subdued; then the silence returns. Just before they leave, their voices get louder and their boots make metallic noises on the stones at the entrance. There are a few more words that can't be heard. The voices withdraw toward the forest, together with the sound of the dull, heavy steps.

But they found nothing. Even though the four foresters searched for days, almost covering the entire chain of mountains, they did not find any trace of the murderers. They did not see any suspicious smoke, nor hear any voices that were not those of the cuckoos, the crows, or the wind. Every so often some rocks rolled down the gray walls that hang over the woods. It was not that they saw the tumbling rocks, for they did not; they heard only the sound of very distant land-slides.

For an entire day Durante followed the upper edge of the forest, firing two shots at regular intervals, one from his rifle, the other from a pistol, to create the impression that there were two men. Mean-while, in a clearing near some old huts, Molo lay in ambush: the brig-ands might hear those shots and come down without worrying about the rest of the woods. But no one was seen. And that day there wasn't any wind, so even the faintest noises could be distinguished.

Molo and Durante came back first, exhausted and without hav-ing had more than a mouthful to eat. The next day, a little before noon, Montani and Fornioi returned. Did they find anything?

"Here's our great catch," says Fornioi, pulling a bird from his bag. It is a fat crow, already plucked.

"A crow? You really don't plan to eat that, do you?"

"Go on, make some soup with this bird."

7

Even Del Colle winds up being forgotten. His famous English shot-gun with the engraving on the barrel passes to Giovanni Marden, who has succeeded him as commander: it is a handsome gun, even if a little old.

Time continues to pass without anyone's notice; it is fall already and many memories have faded away. The man who took his gun from the wall to go out armed at night now leaves it home, hanging on the same nail as before to cover the pale stain. At certain times of the day, the sunlight strikes the weapon, making the steel sparkle. Meanwhile the dust settles; from one day to the next you can't see it, but after a few weeks it has covered everything. It coats books, cor-nices, furniture, even the clock that stands at the top of the campanile in San Nicola. Sometimes, at night, the bell-ringer strains his ears; he seems to hear the clock pant every so often. The panting actually in-creases, making the entire tower resound. Then it gradually grows faint, becoming more and more remote, perhaps borne away by the wind.

Life is serene at the new house. Everything has been carefully arranged; there is even a rack for the rifles with small brass name plates for each forester. Yet no one has really gotten used to it. This was to be expected: it is a new building, with new furniture; the bunks each have a wire netting, whereas before there were only wooden planks. In every room there are oil lamps, the odor of wood, the ticking of the clock. And yet there is something else that no one can describe.

"You can notice that Del Colle is gone," somebody said one night.

But no, this isn't it. The thing is that they all live exactly as if someone were about to arrive at any moment. They are not expecting an enemy's attack, but some person, a stranger; they can't say who. In the meantime the eyes turn toward the towering peaks; they are gray and the gray clouds that pass over them are always the same, always the same.

Every three or four days the guard at the powder magazine is changed. As a rule, the change is made at four in the afternoon, in front of the magazine, near the huge mound of gravel between the walls of the Palazzo and the Polveriera. The three men who have been relieved then withdraw through the detritus and soon disappear.

How ridiculous it is to store the powder here. The workers left it behind when the construction of the famous road was abandoned. Once, while the work was underway, the magazine was justified. But is it now worth the trouble to maintain a special guard detail for so little ammunition? "It's better this way," Marden always says. "If the powder weren't there, some of us would be dismissed."

About fifty meters away from the magazine, on another spur projecting from the rockface, stands the shed for the guard detail. As usual there is a vast silence. From inside the shed, through a small window, you can see the sentry pacing back and forth, his rifle resting on his shoulder; in front of the magazine, down among the stones, lay the remnants of the barbed wire, some old rusty tins, and the curved wooden slats from an ancient powder keg. Each forester has seen this view so many times that it is etched into his memory.

Barnabo likes to spend nights in the shed, especially when he is on duty with Berton and they can chatter away for hours in the darkness.

"Can you imagine if they turned up tonight?" asks Berton, lying on the bunk in front of Barnabo's. "We see them in time and go outside to hide behind a rock. Then bang bang—hands up! We take them all prisoner. Can you imagine what a shock it would be?"

"Give me a match so I can see what time it is," says Barnabo. The other turns in his bunk. You can hear the noise of the matches shaken in the box. Barnabo lights one: 10:30. Then the flame goes out. You can hear whistling outside. It is Montani, taking his turn as sentry.

"Say, Berton, tell me the truth: When you were stationed here the other times, did you always post a guard at night too?"

"Weren't you here before? You know very well what they do. But I don't trust Montani. It isn't that he's capable of being a spy; he just talks so little. Who knows what he's thinking."

"He thinks we're all inferior, that's what. He certainly mustn't feel very comfortable with us two."

"Did you ever notice that—"

"The other day I asked him if he liked the new house. 'Why must I like or dislike it?' was his answer; then he turned away."

"I was going to ask if you ever saw how happy he is when he's on guard duty."

"He can be happy only in a manner of speaking."

Berton sits up in the bed, making it creak. "These damn covers keep sliding off," he says. He rearranges them and turns over on his back, exasperated. Then he is silent.

"Does he have family in San Nicola?" asks Barnabo. "Do you know them?"

"He's never had any family in these parts. It's Collinet who has an uncle."

"Look, I don't understand. Why did Montani have to be chosen for the foresters with so many strong, agreeable men around here? He always has that stern look on his face. He's so efficient, always in good with his superiors, he even humiliates himself. Then take Paolier, for example. It's been two years since he asked to join the foresters. The amazing thing is that he persists. Tell him that it's useless to wait and he gets philosophical. 'Today it's raining, but tomorrow the sky will be clear,' he always answers. And meanwhile they haven't called him. Tomorrow, it's always tomorrow."

Barnabo breaks off because he notices that Berton has fallen asleep. It was as if he were talking to the darkness, to a corpse. There isn't much to say.

Midnight. Barnabo jumps out of bed and grabs his rifle. He tiptoes to the door and opens it very slowly. It is cold and there are clouds overhead.

"Montani," he shouts in a low voice, "you can go to sleep if you want."

He stops in front of the magazine and sits down on the usual rock. Montani is a short distance away but doesn't nod to him.

"Don't you go to sleep?"

"I'm not sleepy. Anyway, four eyes see better than two."

Montani really doesn't trust Barnabo. Who knows what he thinks of him. He just wants to appear zealous, to have some sort of edge over the others. Barnabo is seized with the desire to throw down his gun and leave. But no, he wouldn't be able to rest if he went back to bed. Montani would take him at his word and stay on duty for eight straight hours. That bastard doesn't trust him.

Now it is too cold to stand still. Barnabo starts to pace back and forth. His day will come—by God, it must. The Palazzo and the Polveriera have vanished in the clouds; it is about to rain. But one fine day you will be able to see all these mountains, all the sheer rock walls, and up there, on a peak, a man. It will be a sunny day, a day he will never forget.

Yet this is just a story; he knows it well. Things will go on just as they always have, one year after another, without anyone's notice. Montani walks very slowly toward the shed. "Now even he is sleepy," thinks Barnabo. "Couldn't he have gone to bed before, when we did? But no, he isn't satisfied unless he humiliates someone."

It has started to rain. Montani goes to sleep and Barnabo feels a lump in his throat. He slowly raises his head. He hears the noise of the water on the rocks and on the zinc roof of the shed. Now, alone, he turns his rifle upside down so that the inside of the barrel does not get wet and resumes his pacing. He would like to sing something. The water soaks his face and runs down his cheeks in rivulets, leaving a bitter taste in his mouth.

8

It is the feast of San Nicola. The sun shines on the colored banners strung across the streets. The bells ring loudly in the crisp morning air. The square is filled with foreign merchants and musicians with harmonicas, flutes, and guitars. Through the crowd pass rich carriages that no one has ever seen before. In the church the choir is singing the solemn Mass; the rays of sunlight pierce the smoke from the incense.

The foresters have also come down to the village, except for the three men stationed at the magazine and Berton, who has stayed behind to look after the house. Barnabo was happy early in the morning, while he was going to San Nicola; on a day like this there is always something to amuse a young man. "Let's do this, let's do that": everyone has made great plans. Afterward (as Barnabo is well aware) the others will stop at the inn until late at night. He, however, will go to the shooting range where there is dancing on holidays.

It is almost two in the afternoon. Wearing his new shoes and his hat with the feather, Barnabo walks to the shooting range down those deserted, out-of-the-way paths full of happy sunlight. All of a sudden, he comes upon an old woman in a shady corner; her dog is lying on the ground, constantly moaning. It is a wretched mongrel, turned on his side as if he were about to die. Barnabo stops to look.

"Come on, Moro, buck up now," the old woman says softly to the animal. "Let's go home."

And the dog (the moaning has stopped) slowly gets up and walks, swaying from side to side as if he were drunk. He plods along, and the old woman follows him. The animal is now in the sunlight and turns down a little trail. The woman has also disappeared. Barnabo stops to observe the deserted path. Then he starts walking again. After a few steps he hears the faint sounds of distant music.

At the shooting range there is a large courtyard surrounded by a wall. In front of the entrance, on a stage, stand several young men with guitars, harmonicas, and a mandolin. Barnabo does not recognize anyone. "Maybe someone will come later on," he thinks and sits on a bench. "If I find a girl, I'll dance." Yet he knows that this really isn't a place for a forester. These are wealthy people who live like great lords. Who would pay any attention to him?

The old waltz has changed, become unrecognizable. In the beginning they used to play it on violins, many years ago, in a faraway city. After a long journey the music reached the mountains, but it is weary: you can hear it dragging its feet; all its joy is gone.

Barnabo does not look at the girls anymore. He looks at the green branches in the trees beyond the wall, gently moved by the wind; the distant peaks gleam among the leaves, bathed by the sunlight. On one summit you can still see the beret that Berton nailed there. The feather is hanging by a thread; it dangles in the wind. In a little while, look carefully, you will see it fly away.

9

Berton, in the meantime, has stayed by himself at the new house. He is lying down in the field, in the sunlight, looking at the mountains.

No one has ever been up there and perhaps no one will ever be; but it is amusing to observe them, even for hours on end. From here you can see the Pagossa stretching its uneven chain of summits toward the east.

San Nicola was built hundreds of years ago. The campanile is very old, and several houses are so decrepit that they threaten to collapse. The villagers have built bridges and streets and pushed on into the forest as long as there was wood to cut. But at the edge of the gravel everything stopped. No one has heard the noise of the wind on the highest peaks. From their childhood on, they see the mountains and they have even learned to distinguish them by name, but no one thinks of climbing to the point where the great white clouds stop in the summer. Besides, what would they find there?

Berton continues to look at the mountains. A small cloud crosses the Pagossa; it seems to want to linger, but the wind pushes it away. A gauzy white band remains attached to the peak; it looks like smoke, very pale against the sky. The rest of the cloud is already very far away, but that luminous trail has still not dissipated.

The sun slowly sets. Berton feels the evening approaching. In a little while he has to join some of the other men to relieve the guard at the magazine. In his mind's eye, he walks down the road, passes beyond San Nicola and moves on until he reaches the plain. He is now in a distant village, in front of his own house. His father, who is a carpenter, sits resting in the kitchen. His sister Maria is sewing in another room. After he left, the house must have really quieted down. But he has his whole life ahead of him. Who knows if he will ever have to go back there?

While Berton is absorbed in his imagination, a thin plume of smoke slowly rises from a lofty peak that looks like an eroded tower, just to the right of the Lastoni di Mezzo. It isn't a cloud, but actually black smoke, sketching a column in the sky as if the wind had stopped.

Berton stands up, astonished. It is useless to shout now, to sound the horn or fire warning shots. Someone is in the mountains, where nobody had ever had the courage to go. It is obviously the brigands, the murderers. They have even scaled the tower of rock by themselves.

As the forest becomes more and more shadowy and evening approaches, the walls are aglow with red light. In San Nicola the foresters are drinking and dancing without giving Del Colle a thought. Yes, they had scoured the woods, fired useless shots, patrolled the area for months. But no matter how hard they search, they won't be able to catch anyone who has climbed higher than the ravens.

The shadows have filled the forest and rise over the gravel. The thin clouds fade in the sky. In the valleys it is dark and the nocturnal winds raise their voices. The branches stir. Even the bushes rustle, as they prepare for sleep. The birds' song has stopped.

Berton slowly crosses the field, heading toward the distant peak. The mountains still manage to catch some rays of sunlight; they loom portentously like clouds.

Berton hears his heart beating. He is anxious for night to fall quickly and hopes the other men haven't noticed what he's spotted in the mountains. Besides, the ones at the magazine don't have a clear view. Nobody must know anything about it; perhaps he will mention it only to Barnabo, because he is his friend. Del Colle lies buried in the icy cavern, his shoulders cramped in the narrow box. Darrìo's bones can hardly be seen now that the sun is setting. But all this has remained with Berton. And how he has kept it alive! His colleagues will clearly see it tomorrow morning when they are unable to find him. Where did Berton go? they will ask. Is he perhaps on duty at the magazine? But Berton will not be there, and he will not be on patrol in the woods, nor even at San Nicola. There may be a battle—it seems inevitable. What can you expect?

Yes, he and Barnabo will set out tomorrow morning and vanish among the mountains. The other men will search for them, sounding the horn again and again, but in vain. The sun will make its way through the sky, in the silence of noon, among the afternoon clouds, then set behind Col Verde, but they will not have returned yet. It will be after nightfall and the lamps will be lit when those two emerge from the forest. But why are they so bruised and exhausted? What is that heavy load they carry on their shoulders?

"Rifles," they will answer, "all the brigands' rifles."

Berton is still lost in his imagination when night falls. Cold wind blows through the trees. You can finally hear the voices of the foresters returning from San Nicola, with the usual conversations, the usual laughter.

10

Perhaps this is the day that Barnabo had longed for that night, near the magazine, when he was standing in the rain. Yet now he is afraid. He got up first to show that he is leaving with enthusiasm, but he dashed out at once, hoping for bad weather. The gray clouds from last night still hang over the woods and the clearing.

"I really am afraid," he tells Berton, who has appeared at the door. "I'm afraid the weather will cheat us. That's a storm cloud."

"It's always like this in the morning. Then the clouds disappear when the sun rises. The sky is clear above."

"But do you seriously want to leave in this weather?"

"We can always go under the rocks. Besides, it's early. Go and get your gear."

They depart in the morning fog. The fir branches are damp; a breeze stirs the mist between the trees. Berton walks down the path with a rope slung over his shoulder. He is as calm as if he were going to Mass; he could set out by himself. Barnabo observes the stones on the narrow trail that leads to the magazine. This doesn't seem like the usual way. Those trees too—he has not seen them before.

No one saw them leave or knew where they were heading, so no one can search for them. The path grows steeper. There is a closeness in the air. Barnabo unbuttons his jacket and shifts his rifle from one shoulder to the other. They are now at the upper edge of the forest.

"Look," says Berton, "we have to turn right here and go around the Polveriera."

They soon emerge from the forest; the fog begins to thin out over the rocky slopes. Now they can see the peak of the Polveriera rising black against the brightness in the east, its walls yellow and wet. The air is perfectly limpid, icy, silent. The sun sends out its first glimmer of light. It will be a beautiful day.

So it is no longer possible to think about returning. Barnabo can't wait until they reach the rocks and see how crazy this is. They go farther and farther up in the cool morning shadows, laboriously trudging over the gravel. Every so often they look above. Their climb will take them to the highest crests, over crumbling ridges, past long, dark crevices that pour out frigid gusts of wind. Neither of them can talk.

They have arrived at a huge natural amphitheater. To the left stands the Polveriera, to the right the Pagossa; in the distance, beyond steep rises, they can discern the Lastoni di Mezzo and a part of the tower where Berton saw the smoke. They must now travel straight across a rocky ravine, bounding down one slope in short leaps, then clambering up the other with their hands. The tower gets closer and closer and it turns out to be severely eroded; the rockface is not as straight and smooth as it seemed from far away, but fissured with deep cracks. It isn't so bad. In a little while the sun will rise.

They are on a shelf beneath a sheer mountain wall. The peak has vanished; only the sky above and the drop below are visible. An icy wind blows against them, weakening their resolve. Meanwhile the first rays of sunlight reach the majestic summits. Now Barnabo can see the mountains. They really don't look like towers, or castles, or ruined churches, but just themselves, exactly as they are, with white avalanches, crevices, rocky ledges, and an endless succession of cliffs jutting out over the abyss.

Berton starts the climb, working his way up with his hands. Some stones fall; the butt of his rifle knocks against the rock with a metallic noise. Barnabo stands still, trying to summon up his courage. Why should he risk his life? And yet when it is his turn, he moves, inching up the wall with difficulty. He loses his footing for a moment, but manages to grab on to a spur, his heart beating like a hammer. "It's useless, I can't make it. I knew it would turn out like this."

He will say that he feels sick, that they have taken the wrong trail, but he cannot confess that he is afraid. A nervous tremor passes through his legs, as huge, loose boulders break away and make their long flight downward, silently, before shattering at the bottom with a loud crash. The air carries the odor of powder, of gunshots.

They reach another small shelf, in bright sunshine. Above them stretches an immense wall lined with some cracks; at the top they can see a flue-like groove in a projecting rock.

"Say, Berton, we've taken the wrong way; it'd be better to turn back at this point."

"But we can easily ascend from here. Pull off your boots and you'll see how solid it is. Besides, they can't spot us from the top. Don't worry so much."

Berton goes up slowly, lightly testing the rocks. After a few meters he too trembles as his hands grope for a hold. But he has almost scaled the wall already. And he finally makes it.

"Come on up, the worst is over now," he shouts from above.

Yet after about an hour, they find themselves on a very narrow ledge covered by an overhanging rock. It is clearly impossible to go up any farther and madness to descend. The rock curves out so much that they cannot even find a way to get on it.

"I told you, Berton. Now we're really done for."

The other does not answer; crouched on the edge, he looks down at the now distant gravel. The sun has risen higher without their noticing it. There are gentle breezes. Everything is absolutely tranquil. A few pebbles ricochet off the wall. Before them stand the soaring towers of the Lastoni di Mezzo with their frightening peaks. A small white butterfly flits over the cliffs, occasionally clinging to the rock.

Fear rises from below. The sentry is now pacing back and forth in front of the magazine, illuminated by the sun. A great peace reigns down there on the gravel slopes, an easy, happy life. There is no thought of defeat, of the danger that you may be spotted by the brigands and assailed by gunfire and stones. Barnabo keeps on telling himself that there is nothing more to do. He will end up like Darrìo, like Ermeda. His bunk in the new house will remain just as he left it. A candle end sits on the nearby shelf next to four empty cartridges: he remembers it all very well. Then there is his pipe, hanging from a piece of string.

But Berton starts to whistle softly through his teeth. It is some sort of love song. Come on, Berton, be brave, you still have to get back to the house. He looks at the rocks near them, then ties the rope around his waist, and as Barnabo holds it, lets himself down a few meters. From there he begins to cross over to another part of the rockface, dangling above the immense abyss.

"Hold on, Barnabo, I'm going down now."

He has grasped on to a ledge that he could not even see from above; he is completely absorbed in the effort. Pulled taut over a spur, the rope creaks and vibrates, a few threads snap and blow in the wind. "Now he'll wind up falling," thinks Barnabo. "Your hand loses its grip, you slip backward into the void, then the long flight downward and a terrible scream piercing your brain. There you are, lying in the gravel at the bottom, dead."

It is strange, but Barnabo is no longer afraid. He has now joined the battle. The rope stretches and creaks; Berton has already disappeared over the edge. And yet—wait a moment—there are the tranquil woods in the sun, the solitary road that descends to San Nicola, the evenings at the magazine. You can say whatever you like, but they are still alive. Why should they have died? The rope suddenly gives and slides across the wall, knocking some pebbles loose. Berton must have arrived safely. His happy voice reaches Barnabo.

"Come on, we're here!"

Now it is Barnabo's turn. If he slips, there will be a terrifying plunge before the rope can stop him. But he lets himself down little by little, feeling for the smallest crevices with his feet, unable to see them. Light gusts of wind strike his ears. He can hear his heart pounding.

It is nightfall when they touch the gravel again, a crystal-clear night in the mountains. Their hands are bloody, their clothes torn. Berton bounds down the rocky slope in great leaps. Barnabo heads for the forest, stopping every so often and turning back to look. A flock of crows appears, flying in close formation over the treetops toward the peaks.

In the midst of the black recesses of the forest Barnabo hears a gunshot. A great silence follows. Then he hears the distant echo between the colossal walls. "It must have been Berton, or another forester," he thinks. "Every once in a while they enjoy shooting like that, into the trees, for the sheer pleasure of shooting." But his heart has started to pound again.

One of the crows begins to shriek desperately and lags behind the others, even though he is beating his wings very fast. This was the target. As his companions move farther away, the bird's flight becomes erratic; he is wounded and turns toward the mountain. At times he seems to drop, but then he furiously lifts himself again. He passes over Barnabo's head, still shrieking, and vanishes in the distance. Those eerie calls hang in the air, close to the Polveriera.

As Barnabo goes deeper into the woods, he meets his friend hidden behind some branches: he did not fire the shot. There is a vast silence. They look around among the trees, then back toward the gravel.

"You were foolish to move," says Berton. "If you had stayed there, we might have caught them."

"Who?"

"Bravo! The ones who were shooting. It must have been Del Colle's murderers. Now who knows where they've gone."

"There really wasn't any way we could find them in here. What did you expect? Besides, who told you it wasn't one of our men?"

"Come on, at this hour—"

"It was probably Montani. He often travels around these parts. He says that there are—"

"They've gotten far away by now. But wait, you can never tell."

They are whispering, lying down between the trees with their rifles in their hands. Everything is very calm, just as before an ambush. And yet the wind has begun to blow through the treetops, sending a quiet sound over the deserted brushwood. The wind is amusing himself. He comes from afar and does not stop to look at the men who are hiding there. He encounters the smoke from the gunfire and drags it behind him, lifting it high above the trees and scattering it over the last peaks, solitary as always.

II

The sun serenely enters the windows in the huge silent barns at the foot of the valley, setting aglow the yellow heaps of corn. Above, Barnabo is descending the Polveriera once again; in a little while he will reach the gravel, overcome with delicious weariness. His friend Berton is already running through the loose rock, sending showers of stones down the slope.

Berton and Barnabo have returned from the mountains for the second time, after searching for the murderers. Two days ago they saw another plume of black smoke on the Polveriera. It wasn't a cloud; they had seen it very clearly: it was the same black smoke. And after they had gone on duty at the magazine that morning, they used it as a pretext to head straight for the peak. "We are climbing to the top," Berton said, "so they can't start any landslides down on us."

They found an immense silence. At the base of the Polveriera, they took a very steep ridge that ascended the eastern slope and almost led all the way up. Then things got serious. Of course, none of the foresters had ever ventured that far. Every time Berton climbed up the projecting rocks and disappeared above him, Barnabo anxiously asked himself, "Should we go on? Or would it be better to turn back?"

Thus, meter by meter, they reached the final crest. It was scattered with crumbling rock and beaten by an eternal wind. They waited for interminable minutes in the sun, on narrow ledges, over invisible abysses, listening for voices, looking for some sign of a human presence. But there was nothing.

Under the peak, in a sort of grotto where no one could see them, Berton had finally let out a long shout, one of those sounds that can always be heard in the mountains. But no one had answered. There was the wind, only the wind, whistling through the jagged rocks.

A little later they were on the peak. All that effort and not the slightest trace of the murderers. Yet Barnabo and Berton had felt content; while they were up there, no one could touch them. San Nicola, the other men, everything was very far away. At the bottom you could hardly see the little roof of the guards' shed. It was so incredibly small.

The last fears faded when they were about to touch the comforting gravel. "Berton!" Barnabo had shouted to his friend, who was already some distance away. "Go on to the magazine. Take my gear. I'll come later, straight from the house."

Why rush down? His mouth is parched; a cut in his left thumb is bleeding. There is a stifling warmth in the ravine, which is full of fallen rocks. Yet for the first time Barnabo feels at ease here. The peak of the Polveriera soars into the pale sky. The light is growing fainter. It is now too late to reach the magazine. The guard will have already been changed.

When he has nearly arrived at the last section of the wall, Barnabo suddenly hears a shout, something that isn't new to him. Where has he heard that voice? He remembers: it is the cry of the wounded crow that he heard the other night. In fact, Barnabo manages to see the dying bird on a shelf in the rockface; one of his wings is propped against the wall. He trembles continually, as if he were sobbing. He will soon be dead.

Barnabo has stopped. The sight of that bird has destroyed all the satisfaction he had just felt. He climbs to the ledge and seizes the animal. His wing is bloody, and a shudder passes through his body.

Is Barnabo, who has scaled the summit of that mountain, afraid to kill a bird? With the crow in his hand, he has stopped to look at the overhanging walls, absorbed in thought. He realizes that something is eluding him, and he is unable to stop it. He sees the Polveriera, as on every other night, with the same clouds, the same luminous walls. Barnabo has touched its peak. But what has it gotten him? Where a few hours ago his voice had resounded, he now hears only the wind.

There is a vast silence, in which you can hear distant roars from unknown valleys. The crow has stopped moving. Perhaps he is on the verge of death. Barnabo slips him inside the large back pocket of his jacket and continues his descent. He has changed his mind: instead of going down to the house, he will return to the magazine. It is still early and if they discover his absence, it will mean trouble.

It is around 4:30 in the afternoon. When Barnabo reaches the base of the wall and is about to cross the last ridge before the magazine, a gunshot rends the air, echoing through the valley. Was that Berton shooting? What a foolish way to amuse yourself. Everything happens in a few seconds.

Having passed beyond the ridge, Barnabo sees four men with rifles sneaking toward the magazine. Franze is near the door of the shed, crouched down behind a rock, aiming his gun, but Berton is nowhere in sight. You can see Franze firing shots but missing; three sharp cracks answer him, resounding in the distance.

Barnabo is about to run down when he suddenly stops breathing. About fifty meters above him appears another man, pointing a rifle at his back.

"Don't make a move."

Barnabo's legs tremble. He is speechless. He takes a few steps backward, then throws himself over a ledge. He is paralyzed by fear and is perfectly aware of it, as the shots fill the air around him.

Franze has run out of cartridges. The four men are close by. Two of them hold him at bay, threatening him with shots. The others hurl a huge rock against the door of the magazine, trying to force it open. The shooting has stopped, and in the vast silence the dull thud against the door fades, together with the other voices. The brigands succeed in getting to the powder and after a few moments they reappear with several small sacks, which they hurriedly stuff into their pockets.

Then, near the Palazzo, a cry of alarm rings out. It is Berton coming to help. Who knows why he had left. He runs over the gravel, stumbling. "Stop! Stop!" But at this point nothing can be done. Before he crosses the clearing, the strangers retreat up the rocky slope and start shooting again. "Shoot at them, Berton! What are you waiting for?" shouts Franze, his face flushed. It is useless: the battle is lost. As soon as Berton begins to pursue them, he is shot in the leg and falls. The echoes of the gunfire subside and uncertain voices remain. The brigands are now far away, disappearing among the rocks.

Barnabo, who had stayed behind a boulder, petrified, now feels a tremor shaking his entire body. The danger is over, but he does not have the nerve to move. He is crushed by the awareness that he was a coward. He slowly steps backward, so that his two colleagues cannot see him, and cautiously returns to the path he had left: he will go straight down to the house and create the impression that he was not there when the incident occurred; no one will know what happened.

He wanders through the woods for hours without finding any peace, tormenting himself with the memory, asking himself why he was afraid, but unable to achieve any understanding. Finally (night has already fallen) Barnabo approaches the house. From the outside he hears a tumult of voices. He distinguishes the inspector's; he can see that they have sent for him. Barnabo slowly opens the door: "Good heavens, what happened?"

"Here he is," shouts Franze. "Where have you been, dammit!"

Everyone gathers around. Only the inspector, who is leaning against the wall, and Berton, who sits on a chair with one leg bandaged, stay where they are.

"Ah, the good soldier," says Marden, beside himself with anger. "You have really surpassed yourself this time."

Barnabo takes a step back, feeling his face inflamed, whispering incomprehensible words.

"So you ran away? Were you frightened?" the inspector asks dryly. All the others stand listening.

"But I already told you," Berton intervenes, "I already told you he wasn't there. He doesn't know what happened—"

"Shut up and don't interfere. Let him talk. Well, Barnabo, do you want to answer?"

"But he wasn't there!" insists Berton. "I tell you he wasn't there. What does he know?"

Barnabo forgets his shame and feels a little reassured. So no one saw him run away; no one will be able to make any accusations. He pretends not to know anything.

"Are you going to tell me what happened?"

"It's enough to drive you mad," says the inspector, turning to Giovanni Marden. "There isn't even any way we can make him talk. . . . But it certainly won't end here. It can't be overlooked!"

He moves toward the door, followed by Marden, and goes out into the night.

The worst is avoided. No one knows the truth: that Barnabo fled in fear before the criminals. Everyone thinks that when the magazine was raided, he was far away, hunting, or doing something similar. So he will not be embarrassed. But they may punish him anyway for abandoning his post. The other men plainly tell him what to expect: he will be discharged from the foresters.

12

As on every other night, the foresters are asleep. A little light enters the windows. Barnabo is unable to get any rest. He has suffered too hard a blow. There is no point in deluding himself anymore. Perhaps, if he had insisted, if he had made Marden believe that he had left his post to search for the brigands, he would have been pardoned. But the disgrace has annihilated his will. All the same, Barnabo continues to brood over the incident. Oh, if only at that moment he had been bold, if only he had shot and killed one of the criminals. But it is useless to fantasize. Barnabo will have to bury the humiliating secret inside himself and go on gnawing at his heart. Then an idea crosses his mind: what if the man who had shot at him told the truth? What if, one day, after they had been captured, they revealed his cowardice? A terrible anxiety weighs on him. It would really be better to leave everything and go far away.

In the morning he will be dismissed. They will hand him an envelope with his pay. Then he will be alone with his fate. This was the last night he would spend in the house. His last hours beneath the mountains. It didn't mean much to the other men. It was only idle talk, some laughter, and now he was leaving, chased away like a dog, while they continued to sleep. Someone else will inherit his rifle.

He turns restlessly in bed, hoping to get some sleep. Or at least a little rest. The finger he cut on the rocks is sore. And there is a sharp pain in his chest. Franze is moving now. Perhaps he will wake up and say something to Barnabo. But he doesn't wake up; he is only turning in his sleep, fleeing unknown visions.

Barnabo has gotten used to the darkness and can clearly distinguish the furniture in the room. He can make out the planks in the floor, a chair draped with Franze's clothes, a small package that he does not recognize. His jacket hangs on the wall, a long, suspicious shadow. He hears the faint noises that inhabited houses usually make at night. A creaking door. A window shutter beating against the house. The vague, insistent sound of the wind in the forest. A rat scurrying across the floor and the breathing of the other men, all asleep on this oppressive night.

So he will not see the magazine again. He could go there on his own, but it would only be a deception, a bitter self-delusion.

It is useless to wait for sleep. Barnabo would like to light a candle for some encouragement. But it would only wake the others.

A tormenting groan suddenly breaks the silence.

He recalls that the crow may actually not be dead. He slowly gets out of bed and walks over to his jacket hanging on the wall. He slips a hand into the pocket and feels something warm. The bird is alive.

It is all that bird's fault. If Barnabo had not stopped among the rocks to catch it, perhaps he would have gone straight to the magazine before the raid and, next to his friends, he might have found the courage to act. But now his mind is elsewhere: he imagines the distant world where he will have to go. It appears to him as a broad road with tall white houses and a continuous stream of carriages passing by. A yellow dust rises in the burning sunlight, parching his mouth.

It is a limpid morning with small white clouds rushing through the sky. The other foresters are already out walking through the woods. Sitting on a bench at the door of the house, Barnabo waits for his commander to come and communicate his punishment. In fact, you can see a man emerging from the forest and advancing across the grassy clearing. It is Marden who is approaching; every so often he raises his eyes toward the house. Barnabo does not have the nerve to meet him. Marden arrives, a frown on his face.

"Will you be able to settle down now?"

"Oh, I swear," says Barnabo with a quick smile, his face reddening, "you'll see, I'll put things right."

"I don't mean here, of course," Marden answers icily. "I really hope you aren't deluding yourself. You'll behave somewhere else. Here is your pay. And God bless you."

Marden is about to enter the house when he turns around:

"You must leave the gun, naturally; but you can take the uniform with you, although it is against the rules. Without the badge, of course."

It all happened so simply, just like that.

Barnabo is packing his bag in the deserted room. The crow, which has revived, is perched on a wooden peg driven into the wall, and he seems to be observing, motionless. A stranger had wounded him; he had called for help and now Barnabo must leave.

Barnabo has not touched his bag in two years. The last time he used it was for a long trip he had taken with the other foresters beyond Pian della Croce. He pulls it down from a shelf, full of dust. His steps resound through the deserted room in a new way.

Into the bag he puts his linen, the old velvet suit in which he arrived at San Nicola, but which now has almost turned yellow, then his slippers, the framed picture of the Madonna he had taken from home, his soap, comb, and another hunting shirt he bought a few months back. After half an hour Barnabo's foot locker is nearly empty; all that remains is a couple of ragged bandages, a pack of soiled playing cards, a piece of candle, and the barrel of an old pistol. His memories.

He slowly pulls the string to close the bag. The sky fills with clouds, which from time to time prevent the sunlight from shining into the room. They are moving toward the mountains; the weather may turn bad.

Barnabo wants to leave everything just as if he were coming back that night. The bed with the taut sheets. The candle on the nearby shelf. In fact, his place is now exactly the same as those of the other men, the ones who will return.

Everything is ready. There is nothing more to do. Barnabo has a bitter taste in his mouth. No, you really can't cry on such a beautiful day. He slings the bag over his shoulder.

He was already forgetting something. He did not take his best shoes, which he kept beneath the bed. The oversight did not displease him. He will have a good reason to linger a few more minutes. He opens the window again: if the air doesn't change a little, no one will be able to sleep tonight. A cool, gentle breeze enters the room. The sun is directly overhead, constantly struggling against the clouds. The echo of a song arrives, a very remote sound that does not even seem real. Barnabo has an unpleasant sensation; a slight smile appears on his lips. A fly whirls around him. Everything is in its place, everything is tranquil. This is the time to leave.

Before going down the stairs, Barnabo stops to look back. The row of beds, the squares of sunlight on the floor—it all bespeaks a happy existence.

He would have had to say goodbye to the other men, but they are all gone for the day. They are on duty, of course; there is always the call of duty. Yet someone could have stayed behind. To Hell with them all. He will see them some other time.

Seized by a slight weariness, Barnabo sits down in the ground-floor room. His elbows propped up on the table, he stares straight ahead and does not notice that the crow, which he forgot, has silently come down behind him and perched on his shoulder.

He hears a cheerful voice outside, in the clearing. "Barnabo! Barnabo!" His friend Berton has come back. He appears in the doorway, against a background of sunlight, limping on his wounded leg. He is smiling. "So long, Barnabo."

Barnabo stands up, not knowing what to say, and holds out his hand. "How is your leg?"

Silence. Some clouds have covered the sun.

"Eh, who can say?" answers Berton; then he waits a few minutes. "So where do you think you'll go now?"

"I don't know. I really don't know. To the peak of the Polveriera . . ."

They smile and are on their way out when they stop again. The door—once it was painted green. Now the paint has chipped. Someone has carved in the letters: SAN NICOI. Farther down you can see the marks from the heavy boots; everyone kicks against the door when they enter. The narrow stone steps have worn smooth in a few months and some ants walk over them. Barnabo considers all this carefully, his head slightly bowed.

The two foresters cross the clearing side by side; huge shadows pass over the peaks. They both walk slowly, looking at the ground.

Neither of them has noticed that the crow is following them, flying with difficulty. They do not walk toward the road that goes down to San Nicola, but toward Casa dei Marden. Berton heads in this direction to avoid giving his friend the impression that he is accompanying him all the way; the other because he is not thinking about it.

"How long has it been?" asks Berton in his bright voice.

"Three years. Don't you remember? And it seemed—" Barnabo sighs softly. They are at the edge of the forest. He cannot say a word. He only smiles a little and nods toward a very high peak, which glows in the sun. Then he embraces Berton. Now you can see him walking away.

13

After Barnabo left the new house and entered the forest, he stopped to sit in a small glade. For a long time he looked at the chain of mountains, as the clouds became more dense and threatening. The peaks stood in the distance, motionless and stormy.

He picked up his bag and looked at the immense rocks darkened by the approaching storm, then at the endless woods and the mist blanketing the remote plain. Two paths emanated from that point: one arrived at old Casa dei Marden; the other descended to join the famous road, the topic of so many debates.

After pausing a moment to think, Barnabo took the path to the road. Many clouds had gathered over the mountains, but down below, in the forest, the sun was still shining. He took a few steps, slowly. Only then did Barnabo remember the crow and he turned back to see if the bird might have followed him. But the path was completely deserted. Of course: the crow would remain in the mountains. From that moment on Barnabo continued the descent more rapidly.

They had lined the road with stones. The outer edges had been carefully cut and were maintained by a small embankment. The job was taken seriously. Yet now weeds have sprouted everywhere. Some stretches of the road have already fallen in disrepair.

The way down was pleasantly warm. Barnabo sweated under the weight of the bag. Suddenly his right hand felt for the rifle strap across his shoulder. An old habit.

He would certainly not pass through San Nicola; everyone would ask him annoying questions. So he stopped for the night at an inn near a bridge in the forest. He went inside, but no one was there. He returned to the doorway and sat on a bench. From there you could see only the three peaks of Monte San Nicola emerging from the forest with their bizarre towers. They were very far away; it would take several hours to reach them.

A cart full of logs arrives. There is a huge man who seems to be in charge and two shorter ones, in shirt sleeves, who seem to be woodcutters. They go inside to sit down and start talking loudly. Every so often Barnabo makes out their words. They are arguing about money. Suddenly they begin to laugh. The cart has been left in the middle of the road.

"It started with these American saws," says one of them. "Two years ago. No, it wasn't any more than that. They were expensive. I guarantee you, though, they're the same as ours."

"But what about the temper?"

"What temper, dammit! They're the same thing; I know all about it."

The mountains are now black beneath the gray clouds. Thunder can also be heard coming from afar.

A few raindrops strike the road, leaving spots in the dust. Barnabo gets up, grabs his bag, and is taken to a room. One of the woodcutters who did not see him enter now recognizes his uniform and greets him: "Good evening."

Good evening. Up the wooden steps. Barnabo is not hungry; he throws himself on the bed. Voices reach him from downstairs. A gloomy light enters the room, and the wind stirs the curtains. It will rain hard up there, at the magazine. Barnabo notices his bag sitting on top of a chest. It looks exactly as he had packed it at the new house, three or four hours ago. And yet it seems like much more time has passed. A few hours' walk is enough to distance Barnabo from his entire life as a forester. What is left of all that time? The bag, the uniform, a few other clothes. And then there is the dirt, some pebbles stuck between the nails in his boots. They are fragments of the mountains, remnants of the rocky slopes.

With a desperate desire, Barnabo anxiously searches for anything that can conjure up the past, anything that can recall the great peaks. He even has affection for the cut in his thumb; it was the rocks on the summit that hurt him. He looks attentively at the cut, already dry and closed. How sorry he would be if that sign disappeared too quickly. So he opens the cut again and pulls the skin apart, forcing out a few more drops of blood. Just like two days ago, under the huge rocks of the Polveriera. As the pain returns, it seems as if he has gone back, as if he has pushed back time and is again as he was before, the victorious one who is returning from the unattempted peak. The rain beats noisily on the zinc roof. If only Berton were there to say a few words to him. Barnabo is now sitting on the bed, waiting for the darkness to come.

When he wakes up in the morning, the storm clouds have already left the sky. Through the curtains he can see the sun shining in the nearby woods. He dresses hurriedly, picks up his bag, and stops at the door to see if he has forgotten anything. He will have to travel around fifteen kilometers before he reaches Arboi. From there he will take the train to the home of Giovanni Bella, his cousin, who lives on the distant plain.

A few meters away from the inn, at the point where a path enters the forest, Barnabo notices a black shadow hanging over his head. It is the crow. After having followed Barnabo unseen, painfully beating his wings, the bird waited for him all night on a branch outside the inn, in the storm. The rain had gotten to him and soaked his wings and the wound, which is swollen again.

So Barnabo puts the bird on his shoulder. That sick animal reminds him of the mountains. He too knew the rocks, the interminable walls. What a shame he cannot talk.

The road across the plain, a huge dust cloud, the yellow trees. There is Giovanni Bella's house. An inn stands by the side of the road. Behind it are the stable, the hay loft, a small bakery, and some fields. You can see a low hill close by, and farther on, when the sky is clear, the green mountains.

Over the door of the inn there is an iron plate with the number 846 and the words "Trattoria del Bersaglio." Giovanni Bella is sitting at the table with two other farmers. Someone comes in from the road. It is Barnabo, exhausted by now. Here begins his new life.

14

The peasant's life. In the shade of a walnut tree, on an afternoon in July, Barnabo is hammering a scythe. The metallic noise echoes in the distance. A large white cloud hangs in the east, indicating that much time has passed.

He was not happy in the beginning. He used to wander alone through the countryside for hours on end, and no one could talk to him. Then he adjusted, so much so that he thought about returning to San Nicola one day or another. He often imagined leaving with Berton like that morning and fighting against the brigands. In this way, he started to laugh again and worked the entire day, as the sun faded his memories.

At night the crow perched on a peg next to the window. Sometimes the moonlight entered the room, and the bird's shadow fell across the bed of the sleeping Barnabo. Then the animal grew restless, and if the windows were half-closed, he often jumped down to the windowsill to look at the fields.

One day soon after Barnabo arrived, Giovanni, the cousin who was also his host, had told him:

"Now don't get mad. It can happen to anyone. When I was a soldier, I too was afraid sometimes. It's useless to go on if things aren't right; even the other men's morale suffers from it."

"Afraid? What do you mean 'afraid'?" Barnabo had answered, alarmed. Had the story of that incident reached his relatives as well, and was he suspected of cowardice? He had been so enraged that day that he wanted to leave and show them whether he were still afraid. No one ever mentioned it again to him. Giovanni often told him that he was very welcome at the farm, where workers were needed. Now two years have passed. The foresters never existed. The good days are over, and Barnabo has let them go.

In the beginning he used to search for things that might recall the mountains. He even observed the walls of the houses, mentally comparing them with the great walls of rock. He spent some time contemplating the stones scattered on the ground, easily enlarging them in his imagination and fantasizing very difficult paths of ascent. And yet there were no boulders or cliffs in the fields. The farm did in fact contain a narrow gorge, but it was full of shrubs and plants.

One day, near sunset, he had gone with Giovanni to a shop where they bought tobacco and spices. The heat was stifling. On one wall Barnabo had seen a colored print that represented a little village in the mountains. Any artist who would draw the mountains like that must have never seen them. It was an entirely different world, as were that shop and those fields. Barnabo felt a tightness in his chest; there wasn't enough air to breathe. After he went back outside, on the road, he noticed that he had lost something, but he could not remember what it was. His hand felt empty, and this sensation unnerved him. It was only a few days later, when he was about to enter the Bersaglio, that he realized he had left his rifle.

Then he started to scrimp and save so he could buy a shotgun. After many sacrifices he now has his gun: it is a beautiful single-barrelled weapon with an engraving of a dog. Thus he lets the days pass and sometimes it seems to him that he is happy again.

The days fly by, and already four years have gone. One evening, tired from working, Barnabo goes to his room to rest. Spring has arrived and there is a crescent moon, half veiled by thin clouds. Spring is always like this: you think that you can sleep soundly and then you never manage to sleep at all. Barnabo tosses and turns beneath the covers. The crow's profile is sketched by the faint light of the window. He is asleep on the peg, his beak tucked under his wing, and Barnabo notices that he has changed. Perhaps it is the pleasure of sleeping that makes his feathers thicken that way; and yet they have not done so before. The wake of a distant wind enters the window, carrying the fragrant spring air. A solitary frog continues its harsh singing. As he was watching his crow, Barnabo too fell asleep.

Who knows what that bird has eaten. The next day he is all swollen, and his feathers are dull and ruffled, not black and smooth. In the morning, when Barnabo left for work, the bird did not have the strength to follow him. He leaped down from the peg and whirled around the floor, crying softly.

When Barnabo returns in the evening, the bird is quietly perched on the windowsill. Yet if you look closely, you can see that he has a slight tremor, which shakes him constantly. As soon as Barnabo enters the room, the crow closes his beak and turns his head toward him. The tremor now becomes more intense. Outside the sky is serene, set aglow by the sunset.

It is a tranquil, happy evening. Barnabo has a serious expression on his face; he has stopped to think.

Then, with a push, the crow hurls himself from the windowsill and reaches the branch of a pear tree. From this point, toward the north, you can see the lower chain of the closest mountains: they are crowned with triumphal white clouds frozen in the night air. Stretching his head in that direction, the bird starts to utter long caws. It is the sound he made four years ago, the same one that resounded through the forest after the mysterious gunshot and even climbed the highest walls, echoing in the distance. Perhaps it is the reawakening of some primal instinct; perhaps it is a call to the great peaks, to the remote woods, to friends who have disappeared. All around lie the green fields of some vast plain. You can see the crow suddenly tremble, then start beating his wings, gradually rising into the air and drawing farther and farther away. It is a desperate flight toward the northen clouds. The bird becomes smaller and smaller until it vanishes on the horizon. But that mournful cry continues to echo for quite a while.

When the others have gone to bed, Barnabo sits at a table in the ground-floor room in the light of an oil lamp. It is one of those nights when you seem to feel time passing. On one wall there is a large stain from the humidity; even at this moment it may be gradually widening. Giovanni Bella's cap sits on a bench. A few moths beat against the lamp. You can hear the crickets' incessant song, as an endless whirl of memories returns. Barnabo would be embarrassed if anyone could see him now: not even a woman would spend so much time pondering the loss of a pet. And yet he feels as if he is nailed to the chair; in the middle of the plain, in the silent house, he realizes that he is alone, completely abandoned. There is little to say: that crow had come with him from the mountains and he was the only thing that remained of that life, the only continuation. Barnabo recalls an old road, now overgrown with weeds, that climbs as far as the gravel. The immense peaks tower above, where landslides sometimes occur, making strange noises. He is thinking of them again, in the bright morning sun, in the midst of an extraordinary stillness. He cannot understand why the light from the lamp has not begun to flicker. Still as a statue, he is about to dig up the past. Outside there is a great chorus of crickets. It will last the entire night.

15

One afternoon, while Barnabo was cutting willow branches near the river, he heard a voice calling him. He noticed that his heart had started to pound; he let the knife fall to the earth. He tried hard to identify that voice: who could it possibly be? Then he ran down along the bank, toward a narrow, muddy path. When he emerged from the underbrush onto the edge of the well-tended green field, he saw Berton waiting for him.

After Barnabo embraced his old friend, he could not find anything to say. Berton had not changed: he was always so quiet and happy. He too had left San Nicola, in order to travel abroad with a relative. Like Barnabo four years ago, he too wore his forester's uniform on the journey. His life among the mountains had also ended. But Berton had left by his own choice, and his colleagues had thrown him a party.

Barnabo accompanied him to the house. "I was down there cutting some branches," he explained and smiled, unable to find the old affection. It was his best friend, the one with whom he had climbed the Polveriera; besides, Berton had tried to save him in front of the inspector. And yet there was nothing at all to say: it was just as if they had seen one another last night. At first Berton also did not know what to say. In his dry, tranquil room on that partly cloudy evening, amid the scent of corn and old furniture, Barnabo showed his friend his hunting rifle. In the meantime he had a bed made so that Berton could spend the night there.

Late in the night, after everyone had gone to sleep, the oil lamp was still burning. Barnabo sat on the bench and Berton, leaning against the table next to a jug of wine, related what had happened.

Four years ago, after Barnabo's departure from the foresters' house, they spent days and days in a vain search for the brigands who had killed Del Colle and raided the powder magazine. For the first time the entire guard, together with several gendarmes who had come from San Nicola for this purpose, crossed the great peaks, pushing on through the ravine of the Polveriera as far as the Lastoni di Mezzo and then travelling around Monte San Nicola and beyond to Pian della Croce. They had decided that whether they caught the brigands alive or dead, it was necessary to put an end to the entire affair. In those fall days, amid the undulating fogs, there were noises from landslides in the mountains and some faint calls. But they did not encounter anyone, nor did they hear any suspicious sounds. One day the clouds finally gathered, and the first snow fell.

It was Montani who thought of it: Couldn't the brigands have returned to Casa dei Marden? Couldn't they be going there to sleep at night, after scattering in the woods? Anyone else would have been afraid to spend the night by himself in an abandoned house.

But Montani was not concerned about such things and for a few weeks, every evening at sunset, even when there were already several centimeters of snow on the ground, he went to shut himself up in the old house. Then, after he bolted the door, he started to smoke, without lighting a lamp, and waited.

"Of course," thinks Montani, "they will not come immediately; you have to be patient." But finally one night, around ten o'clock, as he is dozing off on a pile of hay with his rifle, he is suddenly awakened. There are three knocks on the door so powerful that he thought it would collapse. Montani smiles in the darkness. His hour has come.

Positioning himself behind the door, he waits, holding his breath. A voice on the other side says: "I knew I was right, dammit."

Montani stands still behind the door, waiting a few more moments; then he calls out: "Who goes there?"

"It's a good thing someone's here. Isn't this the foresters' house?"

"Don't try anything funny; there's a shotgun pointed at you."

"Come on, open up, I'm soaked."

Yes, it's true: Montani hears the rain rustling in the grass and resounding on the roof. He opens the door.

He then sees a bearded man about thirty years old. The man says that he has come up from Arboi to sell a rifle to the foresters. He calmly sits down on the hay, right in front of Montani, who cautiously keeps the shotgun aimed at his knees. Outside it continues to rain. The words echo in the empty rooms. The flame in the lamp is getting lower and lower.

"Here's the rifle. It's old, and not very pretty, but you can't find such a sturdy weapon anymore. And then what an aim it has: you have to see it in the hands of a good shot."

Montani draws closer to have a look without putting down his gun. But he does not speak. He approaches and stares at the stranger. The reddish light flickers. The right moment has arrived. Montani raises his rifle to the other man's face. "Put down the gun," he shouts, "and raise your hands. Do you think I'm stupid?"

The stranger leaps to his feet with a frightened smile, his arms raised:

"What's come over you? Have you gone crazy?"

"Crazy or not, you stay put till tomorrow morning; then you'll come to the house with me. Now sit in that corner."

Montani grabs the gun. The air is muggy. At this point he is master of the situation. But in the corner the stranger resumes:

"Do you think that I came down from the mountains? That I'm one of the thieves? Have you really gone crazy?"

Montani looks at him and smiles. The plaintive voice issues from the nearly dark corner:

"I wouldn't come here if I were a smuggler. You can see you don't know them, you can see you don't know what kind of people they are. You think I'd be so stupid to let myself get caught like this?

"Keep on listening," continues the stranger, since Montani does not answer. "Now you'd like to toss me in prison. You're a coward, that's what you are." His voice has now changed; in fact, it seems as if he is laughing. The light grows more and more dim.

"About ten days ago I met one of you foresters. But it's useless to talk to an animal like you. . . ." The voice has broken off. The flame in the lamp flickers a few more times, then the room goes dark. Montani shouts:

"Stay where you are, I'm warning you, if you make a sound, I'll shoot."

After a little while, however, the voice in the corner resumes, the same as before:

"Listen. I used to think that if you're with a friend and someone attacks you on the road, you have the right to shoot. . . . Don't you talk?" There is a brief silence. Montani would like to light a candle, but he doesn't trust his prisoner. Now there is also that damned wind, which has started to blow against the door. All of a sudden, Montani is seized with fear. A single word is enough to frighten him.

"Montani," says the voice in the corner, "listen to me."

How does that brigand know his name? The rain grows increasingly violent; it is now roaring on the roof like a cataract. The door heaves against the hinges, creaking wickedly.

"Montani," says the voice, calmly, "let me go. I must continue my journey now. Besides, you can't hit me here. A little while ago I changed my place and you didn't notice it. But I can see you in the crack of the door. And I have a revolver." The voice has gotten louder, and Montani trembles with rage. No, dammit, I won't let him play with me. There is a spurt of flame, and a blast rips through the air, leaving the odor of gunpowder. The voice in the corner laughs serenely.

"You were wrong, I told you. Now you can leave. It's useless to try to reload your rifle. If you make a sound, I'll shoot."

Montani realizes that there isn't a thing he can do. But he won't let himself be killed like this, for nothing. He'll make a move for the door, and then he'll wait for that bastard. The lamp is burning. The brigand silently lit it, holding the revolver aimed at Montani. The forester is already at the door. It slams with a bang, and the light goes out again.

So, until morning, in the fall rain, Montani waited with a loaded rifle to kill the stranger. But nothing happened. In the first glimmer of dawn, old Casa dei Marden was pitch dark. Montani saw the door jump on its hinges, shaken by the wind. And through the air holes he could see the darkness inside. Then, after sunrise, when he decided to enter the house, no one was there.

Montani had seen the same mysterious man several weeks later, when some snow had already fallen in the ravines and on the ledges. Whitened in this way, the mountains were even more quiet. Because of the bitter cold, Montani would have postponed his vendetta until the following spring if he had not noticed some human footprints at the mouth of the gorge near the magazine.

Without saying anything to anyone, he grabbed a handful of cartridges. He went through the woods and past the magazine, then trudged up the rocky slope, made his way through the narrow pass, and descended the other side. It was an immense valley closed off at the base of the Cima Alta. On that side the footprints continued over a ledge.

Then the silence was pierced by a gunshot. Much higher up, two men appeared on a cliff that jutted straight out from the rockface. They were aiming their rifles down below, probably at some chamois.

Montani could not have hoped for better luck. With infinite caution, he managed to climb up a groove in the rock, his hands freezing. Some crows flew around in an unusual way, whistling, as the roar of falling stones was added to the gunshots.

When Montani had reached the height of the two strangers, he was able to see them better. There could be no doubt that one of them was his visitor that night. The other, perched on a dizzying cornice, seemed even more determined than his companion. For some strange reason, after taking three or four shots, he started to hurl off huge boulders which struck the walls and caused more landslides to crash down the mountain with a deafening noise. Yet he had not noticed the forester's arrival.

In order to get closer, Montani had to cross a steep snowy ledge. As soon as he set foot on it, however, an avalanche of rock and ice fell from above. It was pointless to wait for more than an hour in the hope that he could get past the obstacle. When the forester had crossed the ledge, there was another terrible shower of boulders and snow, as if some of the brigands were above him. Then the two men disappeared and Montani found himself on the frozen wall, amid a series of mysterious landslides. It was not until late in the evening, after a tremendous struggle, that he reached the narrow pass through which he had come, exhausted by the intense cold. The entire mountain was swept by muffled rustlings, like the sound of an army seeking revenge.

Had the glorious legendary times returned to the mountains of San Nicola? After Montani's adventure, there was no trace of the brigands. Had they departed for unknown plains, pursued by the winter? Montani did not see them again, although he had returned three times to mount a counterattack. Nothing new happened until the following winter. Then human footprints again appeared in the ravine. Often the foresters' gazes instinctively turned toward the peaks, searching. In the new house, in San Nicola, and in the dairy cottages scattered across the valleys, bizarre stories were told, especially at night, just as after Ermeda's death. On certain days, the clouds formed dense rings around the cliffs, and thin mists were seen rising from the rocky gorges on the most serene afternoons. The people who lived near the mountains gathered to observe the strange sights, and at night, as if revived, the ancient spirits patrolled the edge of the forest.

Berton told his friend about these things. At the end of the story, Barnabo stood up and lit a candle. "Let's go upstairs." The lamp was out. In the darkened room you could hear steps resounding on the wooden stairs and then on the floor above. You could also hear talking: it was a slow, weary dialogue that gradually gave way to silence.

"So long, Barnabo."

After Berton had quietly dressed, he got ready to depart. Before leaving the room, he awakened Barnabo to say good-bye.

"Are you going now? Couldn't you have told me before?"

"There was no point. I have a long journey ahead of me. What did you expect? It might have been better if I left without saying anything. Let's hope we see each other again."

As Barnabo sat up in bed, he was amazed that his friend's departure did not cause him any pain. The light shone brightly through the window. It was a beautiful summer morning.

"Do you think you'll ever go back there?"

"Who knows, maybe when I'm eighty. Goodbye, Barnabo. I'll write to you."

Berton went downstairs. There was the noise of the lock and then steps drawing away on the road, gradually fading in the distance. The silence reentered the house, which was still immersed in morning sleep, while every so often strange whistling calls crossed the countryside.

16

That fall, near the end of September, the decision was made at San Nicola to put an end to the powder magazine. When it was believed that the thieves or smugglers who may have come to Valfredda from the nearby border had left the area forever, the magazine was raided again one evening at sunset. The strangers—there were about five or six of them; no one saw them clearly—managed to approach the magazine unnoticed while Enrico Pieri was on guard duty. They also would have tried to force open the door if Montani, who was in the shed with Durante, had not sounded the alarm in time. The foresters fired a few shots, which the brigands did not answer as they retreated toward the top of the rocky slope. Nonetheless, you could hear an angry shout, as if one of them had been wounded, and a voice—or so Durante swore—hollered from a huge boulder, beneath the face of the Palazzo, "We'll be back in a year!" and other things that could not be understood amid the erratic gusts of wind.

When the commander of the foresters was informed of the incident, he raised the old question of whether it was not crazy to maintain, in such a remote and troublesome place, a cache of explosives for a road that would no longer be built.

The brigands could always return in the hope of stealing some ammunition, as they had already succeeded in doing. Before the winter arrived, there would be time to remove the explosives, take them to the nearest post, and from there dispatch them to other storage areas. If this were done, it would no longer be necessary to keep any foresters at the new house; they could be stationed at San Nicola. The new arrangement would be both less costly and more efficient, since the foresters' house in Valle delle Grave enabled them to oversee only the woods and the nearest roads, whereas from San Nicola they could easily inspect the other areas, especially Col Verde, where the brigands had helped themselves freely without fear of being caught. There would no longer be any reason to maintain an independent guard detail; the foresters, or at least those who wanted to stay on, would become members of the town watch and would live in the same barracks.

After long debates, this was in fact decided. But since another floor had to be added to the watch's barracks to accommodate the foresters, the change was not made for a long time, and another winter passed, bringing very deep snowfalls. The foresters still had to make laborious trips to and from Valle delle Grave to stock the new house with provisions.

The days moved at a snail's pace, but the last turn of the guard at the magazine finally arrived—to everyone's satisfaction. That afternoon Paolo Marden, Molo, and Battista Fornioi headed toward the ravine to relieve Franze, Collinet, and Pieri. It was a day in June; the sky was uniformly cloudy, and the wind blew over the highest peaks, still a little restless.

Apart from their rifles, the three men carried large bags so that tomorrow morning they could take away anything that was still useful; in one of those bags there was also a jug of wine. It was only right to have a small celebration on their last tour of duty.

They arrived earlier than usual. Since none of them was talking and they were a good half an hour ahead of time, the men they were sent to relieve did not hear them approaching. Franze, Collinet, and Pieri were sitting listlessly in front of the shed, smoking. Only one of them was holding a gun.

"Listen: let's play a joke on them," Molo whispers to his companions when they reach the rocky spur at the base of the magazine. "Stay here." Molo loads his rifle, smiling, then very slowly sneaks up behind the three men on duty. When he is about ten meters away from them, he fires a shot into the air: "Stop or I'll shoot!"

Franze and Collinet leap to their feet as the shot echoes through the ravine. Only Pieri realizes at once that it was a joke and he turns to them, laughing. "Can you believe it?"

"What stupidity," shouts Collinet, white as a sheet.

"Hey, you dog, you were really frightened, weren't you?" Molo laughs scornfully, very satisfied with the result. He slides an iron rod into the barrel of his rifle: the cartridge case doesn't want to come out.

"Well, we can leave now," says Pieri, entering the shed. Then he reappears: "We can carry these two pots down with us; that new one should be enough for you."

"So long," shouts Marden a little later to the three men who are about to leave. "Tell the others to get up early tomorrow morning. It's going to take some time to carry down the powder and everything else. If we don't start early, we won't finish it in a day."

There is the noise of their walk across the gravel, and then the crush of the loose stones grows fainter, as on so many other occasions. Molo, Marden, and Fornioi are now alone. Night is gradually falling, helped along by the clouds. They hear some vague sounds resonating off the rock walls for some strange reason. It must still be the echo of the gunshot that was fired a little while ago.

Thin mists slip between the highest cliffs of the Palazzo. "Look at that peak," says Fornioi, pointing to a spire of rock that suddenly appears amid the clouds. "Last year it wasn't there. The way the mountains change from one year to the next seems so impossible."

"What do you mean 'change'?" laughs Molo. "The peaks aren't made of earth, you know. What happens is that the clouds cover the rockface and usually you can't see it."

The silence is broken by some deep rumbling that reaches the gray walls from far away: perhaps it is thunder, perhaps the noise of sliding boulders. A light shines in the little window of the shed. Marden has lit a fire and is cooking the polenta.

"Look how dark the rocks are tonight. I bet it's going to rain," says Fornioi, sitting on a stone next to Molo in front of the magazine.

"Let's hope the weather doesn't change, at least not until tomorrow night."

This damned magazine. This is why they lost two days every week. They could never go down to San Nicola; there was always the risk that something might happen. There was never any peace. But it is finally over; all that remains is to spend the night.

"It's always this way," says Fornioi, "when there's some boring detail. If something like that comes up, they always call me. Right up to the end, even tonight."

"Well, you can stop worrying about it now: this rotten job is over. Tonight is the last time, just think of it."

"I don't know," says Fornioi. "I remember the day I finished my stint in the army—"

"By the way, is Berton going to come back? Did he say he had to return?"

You can hear Marden's voice coming from the shed. He has started to sing. The mountains have turned black and are fading among the clouds, which still glow a little.

Fornioi and Molo are quiet. In the great silence they hear their colleague's song as the firelight flickers in the little window. Then the voice breaks off.

The nocturnal wind has already awakened, but Molo and Fornioi remain in front of the magazine. The noise of the gusts blowing against the crest of the Palazzo reaches them. For many years, that same sound has heralded nightfall. All the foresters are familiar with it, and no one pays any attention now, although sometimes it resembles a human shout. Well, tonight let it get everything out of its system. Tomorrow no one will be there to listen to it. Tomorrow night there will be no song on the rocky slope of the magazine, no light in the shed. Later on the rain will start to seep into the roof, the first drop will strike the floor, and the beams will rot.

"Shall we go and eat? Or do you want to wait a little longer?" shouts Marden as he comes out of the shed. His two companions stand up and approach the door.

"Now that we've eaten," says Fornioi a little later, "one of us should stay outside. It'd be stupid to take any risks, even on the last night."

"Holy Madonna, what nonsense," answers Marden. "Wait until we have a drink first. After all, it's the last night; we can celebrate a little, it seems to me."

"Celebrate? What do you expect to do with three of us?" says Fornioi. "You can't have a good time up here. . . . Well . . . give me a drink; at least it'll warm me up a bit."

The jug is already empty. The fire burns very brightly because there is plenty of wood to use up. Fornioi has gone outside. The other two warm themselves by the flames. Marden quietly smiles, mulling over obscure thoughts. With an iron rod Molo snaps an incandescent branch already consumed by the fire.

There are still a few logs to burn, but the flame gradually dies down. No one bothers to feed it. In a little while there will be only a few charred pieces of wood, they will hear some crackling, and a thin column of smoke will remain.

They had thought that it would be a beautiful evening, a special evening. Even Fornioi, for all his complaints, was content. There was no denying that only in that solitude, during nights on guard duty, was it possible to talk of certain things. And then there was the pacing back and forth before the magazine, alone, thinking that everyone was asleep, hearing the sound of landslides in the mountains, thinking that it is really the last time, that soon the dawn will arrive and everything will be over. But there was nothing beautiful about it, no satisfaction at all. Molo has gone to bed, but no matter which way he turns, he can't get any sleep. Fornioi too: he has gone outside to tell Marden something, but he doesn't know where to begin.

"Say, Marden, you know what they should do?"

"What?"

"Give us all a few days' leave." Then he tries to laugh.

"And what would you do after?"

The conversation breaks off; the vast silence returns.

"Did you hear that?" says Marden. "Did you hear that whistle a few moments ago? Do you think someone is coming from the house?"

"A whistle? It must have been a bird. One of those . . . what do you call it?"

"The Holy Ghost! Do you think I'm so stupid?"

"But why are they coming here at this hour? It must be almost ten o'clock."

"I don't know anything. I just heard the whistle."

An icy wind blows down from the ravine, making them shiver.

"I hope it's not some sort of surprise! I'm going to put out the fire."

The night passes hour by hour. Molo has continued to sleep. Outside the other two foresters sit up against a boulder, numbed by the cold; they have forgotten their turns as sentry and keep watch together. The very first glimmers of dawn gradually pick out the motionless figures and glance off the barrels of their rifles.

"Here it is," says Marden, shaking his head. "Were you asleep too?"

"It would've really been foolish to waste a night like this and not get any rest."

They stand up, trembling from the cold, and start for the shed.

"In short, even this . . . ," says Marden, staring at the stones on the ground.

"Even this what?"

"Ah, nothing, I was just talking."

A little later you can see Molo leaving the shed. He stops to open the breech of his rifle and works a stick into it. Beneath the overcast sky, billows of wet fog pour down the rock walls.

17

After Berton's visit the previous summer, the breath of the mountains had passed over the fields of the Bersaglio. Perhaps without noticing it, Barnabo had been led back to the transit of time. The torment of certain evenings had returned. He stopped watching the travellers leave the Bersaglio very early in the morning and head straight down the road to the border. The forgotten shame had been revived in his heart. He had taken refuge in the country, in the fertile plain, and perhaps it was his lot to pass his life languidly, in a pointless wait. Berton's visit had suddenly made him realize how many years had passed, and seized by happy memories, Barnabo had often thought that he might go back. Then, from one day to the next, the hope had paled, and the mountains, the Polveriera, the Valle delle Grave had again dissolved in a fog, like things that had never existed.

But the happy day really came. In the following year, one afternoon in July, Barnabo received a letter from Berton. His friend had not forgotten him. Within three days, he wrote, after a year abroad, he would return to San Nicola to take care of some business. Around noon the train would pass through the station at Vogo, not far from the Bersaglio.

"Meet me there. Come with me to San Nicola. After five years everything will be forgotten. You will see: we will be happy."

When they brought him the letter, Barnabo was mowing hay. A new light of contentment was diffused through the fields. So: is Berton making him return to San Nicola? If he wrote, it means that Barnabo will be able to rejoin his old colleagues and become a forester once again; he will resume his life beneath the mountain sun.

Leaving his fellow workers without a word, his scythe over his shoulder, Barnabo heads toward the house. No one calls him or asks him why he is leaving. They follow him out of the corners of their eyes, as the blades flash arcs through the grass.

The sun has still not set. In the deserted kitchen you can hear the harmonious flies, and the creaking chairs talk to one another because they know that no one is there. But now Barnabo's steps resound on the old wooden stairs. The noise fades toward the roof.

Up in a corner of the attic, he rummages through a trunk, looking for his green forester's uniform, his heavy boots, the bag, and all the other things he took with him from the mountains five years before. The bag has not been opened since that day. Barnabo wanted to leave it just like that, so when he came across it again, he would have the illusion that time had not passed. But now, taking it in his hand again, seeing all the dust, feeling the dry canvas, he could not overlook the void that the years had opened in his life.

The moths had eaten holes in the pants to the old uniform. Barnabo doesn't have the nerve to get them mended by the women in the house, so he tries to fix them himself, staying up till late at night with needle and thread, working in the light of a candle. Before going to bed, he puts everything in order as on the eve of a departure.

And in fact, three days later he departs. He takes all his savings with him, as well as the gun, with some cartridges. He is dressed just as he was five years ago, in the green uniform (slightly worn) and the bright hat with the little feather. It has been quite some time since Barnabo was this happy; his heart is filled with hope. When he leaves the Bersaglio in the morning, he does not even turn back to look at the peaceful countryside.

The train stops in the little station at Vogo; the noise fades in the languor of noon. Some scattered voices remain here and there, as in an empty room. Faces look out the windows, a pale cloud hangs in the sky, the shadow of a rifle is cast on the ground. He has still not seen Berton, and the train is going to leave shortly. A few men come out of the station and head down the sunlit road. Barnabo calls his friend, but his shout is hoarse and echoless. Another day. Life continues to pass, but Barnabo feels left out, like something superfluous. Still, it is useless to turn back. Things will brighten up. He climbs into an empty compartment. The heat is unbearable, and there is a foul odor. A subdued singing comes from the open door.

The wheels start to creak, the whistle blows, the station moves, the houses, the fences pass by, and then the trees in the fields start to fly past impetuously. Barnabo begins to regret his decision to return. What is he going to do by himself in San Nicola? Shouldn't he rather be ashamed? But he has no time to think. Looking up, in the corner of the compartment, he sees Berton asleep.

"Good heavens, hello! It's a good thing you got into the same car—and without even seeing me."

"Did you see me come?"

"OK, I did, but . . . but forgive me, why did you wear your uniform?"

"What? I thought that—"

"What an idea! What's gotten into you?"

"You told me, it seems to me."

Then Berton tells him what has happened, how everything has changed at San Nicola, how the foresters have joined the town watch, how they have abandoned the magazine and may have already left the new house. So there is no point in even talking about becoming a forester again.

Barnabo does not answer. Indeed, he was stupid to think otherwise; it was all his fault. He had deceived himself once again. There is always some new hitch. And, now, how will he look to the other men, dressed like that? Wouldn't it be better to turn back? To get off at the next station, to content himself with the tranquil life in the fields of the Bersaglio?

Yet Barnabo continues the journey without even knowing why.

18

The foresters of San Nicola, who have already cleared out of the new house and are temporarily quartered in the barracks of the town watch, see Berton enter the dining room one Sunday accompanied by Barnabo.

Only now does Barnabo realize that it would have been better to stay in the fields. How hard it is to answer the hundreds of questions, to create some pretext to explain why he has come, why he is wearing the uniform. But everyone welcomes him cordially. It seems that they are his friends, that they really never suspected his cowardice.

Marden, who has grown very old, is one of the first to greet him. "Well, look who's here. Where are you coming from?"

Barnabo then relates his life over the past few years, trying to appear unself-conscious as his old companions gather around him. Every so often he glances at the window from which he can see the street and, farther on, a group of fir trees beneath the bright midday sun.

"Do you still wear your uniform?"

"I told him about it." Berton intervenes to spare his friend any embarrassment. "He wanted to come up to hunt. Old clothes are always best if you're travelling through the woods and the mountains."

They begin to talk about hunting. No one takes any particular interest in Barnabo. The foresters don't seem to mind the change in their lives. They talk about the usual things: the inspector's wife has died, the village is building a new church, the price of meat has gone up, the workers from a firm that has bought a huge piece of the forest have arrived. The profit to be realized from this venture is calculated and debated. The area that the town has sold extends almost as far as the new house. This is the topic that Barnabo was waiting for; he wants to talk a little about the new arrangement to know whether it is really impossible to join the foresters again, but without disclosing his motive. The fact that the others have not suspected his cowardice and have perhaps forgotten the episode at the powder magazine gives him new courage. Must someone stay at the new house?

"Indeed," answers Marden, "it will be necessary to find someone."

"Here's an opportunity for you," says Molo, turning toward Barnabo, and then he bursts out laughing.

"What about it? What's so funny? I could easily do it," says Barnabo with a forced smile.

"You're just talking," insists Molo. "I'd like to see you stay up there a month by yourself. Not even I would do it, no matter how much they paid me. You think it's a game? There isn't a dog in those parts."

"He won't really be alone," says Marden, "only in a manner of speaking. First of all, he would be able to come down from time to time, if only to stock provisions. And one of us always turns up in that area."

"But in the end, I say, in the end—"

"And we too must return to the magazine"—it is Franze who is talking now—"near the end of September, the 25th or 26th, I've marked it on the calendar. Then we'll see whether those men from Valfredda will come back. How can they know that the magazine is empty now?"

"You always bring up that stupid story. Who cares whether or not they know about it."

Now everyone remembers. Had not one of the brigands threatened last fall to return and raid the magazine? We shall see them again in a year, he said, and in fact, it was precisely at the end of September.

"As for me," says Marden, "I say we should go. If worst comes to worst, we could turn back. But, by God, they deserve a lesson. . . . By the way, you have had some dealings with them, haven't you, Barnabo?"

Couldn't Marden keep quiet? Barnabo feels everyone's eyes on him and he can't think of anything to say. Let them all go to Hell. They wouldn't get any pleasure from tormenting him if he left now.

But when the sun sets and they all go out into the street, Barnabo feels happy. Marden had really been serious about offering him the job of custodian. The solitude does not frighten him now. He drank a few glasses of wine, and his head is spinning. He confusedly notices the peaks, at the top of the valley, in the beauty of the evening. "By God I'm going there," he murmurs to himself and is seized with a great desire to sing.

So once again Barnabo's life has changed. They have entrusted him with the care of the new house, at least until winter. Marden has called him into his office and turned over to him everything that remains in the house.

"Here is the list. If you like, I can accompany you there, and we can check everything together. If you trust me, you can simply sign here."

Barnabo would have liked for them to go along: they could keep him company, at least for the first night. But he was ashamed to say so. And it would look as if he didn't trust Marden. He picks up the pen and signs.

"Here are the keys to the door. In the table drawer you'll find the keys to the other rooms."

"Excuse me, Marden, but can I have some cartridges?"

"For what? To go hunting? Well, come here and let's see."

Barnabo receives twenty cartridges. Then Marden escorts him to the door.

"So long," he says, shaking Barnabo's hand. "Stay alert. We shall see you again in September, they already told you, I think. It must be the 25th. Besides, in a few days you will be coming down, won't you?"

Having gotten his supplies ready, Barnabo (it is still morning) goes to say goodbye to Berton, who is sleeping in a farmer's house. When Barnabo enters the room, he is still in bed.

"Didn't I say you'd get your job back?"

"I've come to say goodbye. I'm going up at once."

"So fast. But we'll see each other again. Before November. I'll have to come back to take care of some business."

Barnabo feels that he has many things to say. But this is not the time. He shakes Berton's hand and nods to him, smiling slightly.

19

When Barnabo again saw the mountains from nearby, he was not in the least amazed. He stared at the eroded vertical walls, touched the tree trunks, and listened to the familiar noises with pleasure. Nothing had really changed.

He climbed a path overgrown with weeds, his head slightly bowed as if he had taken it every day. He felt that he had known every corner of the forest for an eternity. The branches that grow slowly over many years, then dry up and fall to the earth covered with bright little leaves; the usual birds that come to sing; the occasional passer-by—it has always been this way beneath the mountains.

Here is Casa dei Marden. It has grown much older. One distant morning Giovanni Del Colle lay on that corner of the clearing, killed by a gunshot. Just beyond was his harmonica, damp from the night air. One tree still has the broken branch where Barnabo had hung his hat that memorable day.

All of a sudden, Barnabo emerges from the forest and faces the gravel that collects in smooth mounds at the base of the walls. Then he sees the reddish ravine of the Polveriera, which absorbs all the sun's quiet warmth. Above, a group of peaks rises black beneath an umbrella of clouds; long grooves are etched into the sheer rockface.

Everything is in order at the new house. Barnabo arrives in the afternoon, when the sun is still high. Inside he finds a musty odor. He throws open the windows; the light, which was no longer used to entering the house, is ill-prepared and casts some unpleasant shadows. It is all in order, but much too empty. The room on the second floor with the stripped beds makes a certain impression on him. In accordance with the orders they have given him, Barnabo must make three or four of them; it is not unlikely for the foresters to arrive and spend a few nights here. Indeed, he must call them foresters now; they are no longer his colleagues. Later he goes out into the clearing; it is certainly a beautiful day. There was a time, he thinks, when I would have been afraid to stay here alone, in the middle of the great woods. Yet now he feels calm and is reassured when he notices that the forest too has not changed, not even those special places he knew so well.

It has turned cold. Barnabo goes back inside the ground-floor room, which is completely covered with firewood. When he prepares the logs for the fire, he glances through the window at the chain of peaks, still illuminated by the sunset. He feels the night slowly descending on the house. The wind makes long moans. He hears a distant cuckoo.

He sits by the fire. He used to think that he could finally find some peace and resume the beautiful life he once enjoyed. But now he no longer feels calm: he continues to wait for something, as he has done for many years. It must be coming on September 25th. His day will arrive.

Without much difficulty Barnabo has gotten used to staying alone. Besides, a woodcutter who lives just above San Nicola passes by the house every morning and night. He is about forty and very tall, a quiet, well-meaning fellow who works all day long. Sometimes Barnabo hears the blows of his ax from afar. He gives him a glass of grappa at night, and they exchange a few words.

Every so often, when flocks of crows fly through the forest (they generally come from Col Verde, on their way toward San Nicola), Barnabo sends out a long, modulated whistle, the same sound he used to make when calling his wounded pet. Who knows whether that crow died or found his way back to the mountains. But the birds continue their massive flight over the black forest, cawing in the distance.

Everything has remained as it was before, but it isn't the same. No matter how hard he tries, even on the most beautiful days, Barnabo is unable to find the beauty of certain mornings when he was a forester.

The sun rises behind the Polveriera and sets behind Col Verde. The days are all the same. Listening to the advice of the woodcutter, Barnabo has begun to make wooden spoons; he also amuses himself by carving puppets, which he plans to paint in the various colors he bought at San Nicola. He could even make some money.

In the morning he shaves, polishes his boots, goes to the nearby spring to get water, washes his linen and hangs it up to dry, then makes breakfast. He is now trying to play the harmonica, as the thunder roars beneath the black clouds over the Pagossa. A few drops of water fall here and there, striking the zinc roof with a slight resonance. Later on he hears some voices coming from the direction of Valle delle Grave. It is Battista Fornioi with a stranger who has received permission to hunt. The latter is a rather corpulent man about fifty. He seems satisfied with the walk: "This is a beautiful place," he says, "a beautiful place. Sometimes even I think of coming to live in these parts." He leans his double-barrelled gun in a corner of the room and tosses his bag on the table. Fornioi says little, as usual.

"Can you make us something to eat?" the stranger asks Barnabo. "How about some soup? As quick as you can, please."

At first Barnabo does not answer. He has turned slightly pale.

"Soup?" he then asks, coolly. "You'd like some soup?" He feels Fornioi's expressionless eyes on him. Through the door he sees that the
forest is growing darker, and he makes out the familiar refrain of a
cuckoo lost in some unknown valley. Then he slowly turns around,
his eyes fixed on the floor, goes to pull out the pots and, lighting the
fire, smiles.

The next morning Barnabo must wake up at five to make coffee
for the "gentleman." Fornioi and the stranger depart, heading toward
Col Verde. The storm the night before has not yet passed, but it has
nonetheless left the sky serene. A little later Barnabo also takes his rifle, locks the door of the house, and climbs toward the gravel.

This morning resembles the one when he set out with Berton that
first time to search for the brigands on the unexplored tower. Today,
too, his fears dissolve as he approaches the peaks. Barnabo feels as if
he has become another man; he is almost unable to understand how he
could have acted so cowardly that day.

Even when he arrives at the ravine of the Polveriera and sees the
little shed, now rotted and gray, and the walls of the abandoned magazine, even when he hears the crumbling rocks falling above him, no
tremor passes through his legs.

There is a grave-like silence. It has muffled the wind. The peaks
seem more motionless than usual, as if they were waiting for someone. Why has Barnabo gone up so far? Isn't there a chance that he
might meet the brigands from Valfredda and be killed? Yet none of
these thoughts frightens him.

Barnabo snaps a wire and manages to unfasten the door of the
shed. He flings it open with a bang, making the shed resound like an
empty chest. The disjointed hinges creak sourly. A bright light penetrates the cracks in the roof and the uneven planks nailed across the
little window. The foresters left some weeks ago, and the shed has
been empty for quite a while. He imagines how time passes in that
room without the slightest sound, how the morning sun shines
through the cracks and slowly sends its rays across the floor. He thinks
of the noise made by the rain on the zinc roof, the force of the wind
against the door, the disconsolate nights.

In the sunny ravine, his rifle resting on his shoulder, Barnabo
starts walking back and forth before the magazine as if he were on
guard duty. He is amusing himself by trying to reproduce his past

faithfully. In this way, he seems to push back the years for a few moments. Then he has the feeling that the peaks can see him. He resumes his march toward the far edge of the ravine.

The signs of the usual life end, and the rocks begin to rise, first streaming with pebbles and then, as they mount higher, perfectly bare. Climbing up by easy leaps, Barnabo suddenly comes across an abandoned rifle on a narrow ledge. The weapon seems to be in working order, but the trigger is broken and the butt chipped, perhaps because of a fall. Against the white gravel on the ledge, it first looked like one of those walking sticks you sometimes find scattered through the mountains, like the mysterious pieces of wood that Darrìo had often carried to Casa dei Marden, the remnants of his bold peregrinations. The rifle must have been there just a short time, since there is no trace of rust. Something strange passes through the silent, tranquil air.

Later, when the sun is at its brightest, Barnabo reaches the narrow pass and sees, past the deep valley crowded with stones, the Cima Alta lifting its peak to an incredible height; the walls facing west sink into a vast hole, and the rays of sunlight that shine across them pick out some rust-colored crevices. To Barnabo's left looms the north wall of the Palazzo, black in the shadows. A little lower begins the ridge where Montani had ventured in the late October snow.

20

Time seems to take so long to pass and then it flies like the wind. The end of September has now arrived at the mountains of San Nicola. The weather has been beautiful so far, although the peaks have a different color. For several days now, Barnabo has fixed his gaze on the crests of the Palazzo and the Polveriera. Tomorrow is September 25th; the brigands from Valfredda are expected to return. They swore that they would make another raid, so tomorrow all the foresters (although you never know) will again meet at the house to send a guard detail to the abandoned magazine. Barnabo wants to go with them.

When the sun rises, flaccid clouds hang in the sky. Barnabo wanders through the forest looking for mushrooms. He must prepare a first-rate supper because the foresters will arrive at nightfall. All his sadness has disappeared. For a few hours, finally, he will no longer be alone and he will be able to show—in fact, he *will* show his old colleagues something. As usual he is brooding over the past again, and his shame is renewed. Every time he thinks of the incident, his mood suddenly changes; he feels a burning in his chest. Nobody saw him run away from the brigands, nobody will ever know anything about it, and yet in front of the foresters he always winds up lowering his eyes. But tomorrow, finally, there will be a great volley of shots and he will lead the way.

He sets the table with great care, cleans the wine bottles, spreads some branches, and lights a huge fire to cook the polenta. It is four in the afternoon; the entire valley lies in silence. Gray clouds gather over the peaks and grow more and more dark. The guard detail will arrive late in the day, at suppertime.

Around five o'clock the rain starts to fall. At first it seems nothing more than a drizzle, and yet in a few minutes everything is soaked. Half an hour later Barnabo, who is working near the fire, hears his name shouted from the woods.

It isn't the foresters, but the woodcutter, that hardy fellow who resembles a priest. He has gotten a bad cut on his hand and asks for a bandage. Barnabo feels the humidity invade the house; the peaks, from which he has not taken his eyes, have darkened.

"It isn't for me," says the woodcutter, "but if they see me come home with this wound . . ."

"Give me your hand. I've found a bandage. But first we have to clean it."

Barnabo helps him clean the cut and bandage his hand.

"Why don't you stay the night? People are coming, as you can see."

"I wanted to ask you why you're going to all this trouble. Who is the feast for?"

"The foresters are coming. By the way, you can taste something for me."

"I'm here to help if you need me."

There is a moment of silence. The rain falls harder and harder. Some wood crackles in the fire.

"No, it isn't necessary," says Barnabo. "Yet now that I think of it . . ."

"Go on, tell me without all this fuss."

"No, it's nothing. Something just crossed my mind. And . . . so do you want to stay?"

"You're kind, but they're waiting for me at home. And then"— here he starts to smile—"these things are not for me. Maybe another time. And thanks; I forgot to tell you."

The woodcutter disappears in the darkness. The water is pouring down in buckets; it is raining fiercely. The campanile at San Nicola has already struck six. Barnabo has begun to make the polenta. In the light of the oil lamp the windows appear black. Every so often Barnabo leaves the fire, goes to the door, and sends out a long shout, one of those that can travel a great distance, but only the rain answers him. Why are they so late? The meal is going to be ruined.

The hands of the alarm clock that sits above the fireplace continue to turn. It is now 7:45. The rain has subsided, but some drops still beat on the zinc roof. The polenta has been put on the table, and the steam slowly rises from the pot. Barnabo is sitting beside the fire; he seems to be still waiting, his eyes fixed on the floor. Then finally he understands. Little by little the whole thing dawns on him: it was all a beautiful joke. He imagines that the foresters are down at San Nicola, merrily eating their supper and laughing at him, thinking that he is afraid. It was really a brilliant idea. And as on that distant night at the magazine, in the rain, Barnabo feels something heavy and bitter rising in his chest. But now he suddenly raises his head. Someone is approaching; the door opens.

What a foolish hope. It is only the woodcutter; he had forgotten his bundle of wood.

"I didn't even remember," he says, looking around, "that tomorrow is a holiday. Ah, here it is."

Having gotten together his bundle, he is about to leave again, but near the door he turns back, as if he had recalled something.

"Say, Barnabo, didn't they come?"

Barnabo stares at him without moving from the chair, his back bent forward.

"I did everything," he slowly answers, "everything . . ." His voice breaks off. A lump has closed his throat. But the other man does not understand. He smiles and touches his hat.

"Well, I must be going before it gets too late. I'll see you Monday again."

He leaves. His steps resound on the porch and draw away, splashing across the clearing. The flame flickers in the lamp; only a few embers glow in the fireplace. Then a sudden tremor shakes Barnabo; he springs up from the chair, muttering confused words in the empty room. He seizes the tongs from the fireplace and strikes the table with a horrible blow, cracking a dish in half. Something had been building and building inside him for a time, and now he bursts into a rage. He beats the tongs against the wall like a madman, grazing the lantern, which falls to the floor. Then he stops, panting with terrible anguish.

The lamp suddenly goes out. Everything is black. But no, not everything. You can still see a little. Barnabo stands petrified: through the window, in the midst of the pitch darkness, he notices the glimmer of a distant light. His hand slowly opens, and the tongs fall to the floor with a heavy iron thud. Stumbling in the dark, he runs to the door and heads out across the clearing; high in the mountains, on the towering rocks of the Palazzo, there is a very remote fire. Have the brigands really returned? Are they camped on the cliffs, waiting for dawn to descend to the magazine? Sudden gusts of wind pass over the nearby woods. The foresters thought that the brigands were joking, but they have kept their word.

The humid air of the valley has filled the house. Barnabo goes back into the room, feeling a new serenity. Then a melody crosses his mind. The music is old; it recalls the good times and resembles those marches that were popular many years ago. Barnabo stays in the dark room, leaning against the table, and softly sings the song, whistling between his teeth. The melancholy air has a military strain in it. "Tomorrow we must depart, and head for faraway lands. The first four have had their start, and left behind morning's sands." Meanwhile Barnabo's eyes pierce the window, trained on the peaks, on the distant, solitary light.

The mysterious light on the rocks of the Palazzo goes out a little later, and everything is dark until the clouds part and the stars become visible. Barnabo has thrown himself on the bed, completely dressed, his hands clasped behind his head, and he stares into the mass of trees that blacken the window. He feels, like never before, the closeness of the mountains, with their deserted valleys, dark gorges, sudden landslides, with the thousands of ancient stories and all the other things that no one could ever describe completely. Soon fall will begin, and in the winter the snows will come. Then there will be the warm sun, the bright light of spring on the scented woods. The birds will sing again, and at night you will hear the voices of men who hope for better things. But now the strangers from Valfredda are in the mountains and they plan to loot the area. Darrìo's bones lie beneath them, on a ledge in the immense walls, drenched by the rain; at the base of the cold gorge where the waterfall rushes, Del Colle's body is buried with the bullet that killed him. The foresters are sleeping down at San Nicola.

Barnabo, lying motionless in his bed, has still not closed his eyes; it is impossible to say what he may be thinking. You can hear only his quiet breathing, as if he had been freed from every anxiety.

Behind the Polveriera a glimmer of light finally appears. Everything is perfectly tranquil; the clouds have fled, leaving the sky limpid, and a cold wind passes over the forest in long gusts. Bathed by the storm, the peaks still repose in the nocturnal shadows; they seem much larger, fine as crystal. Without lighting the lamp, Barnabo has gotten out of bed and gone downstairs. He takes his rifle from the rack and puts some cartridges in his pockets.

He opens the door and sees the trees stirring in the wind. The air is extraordinarily light. He closes the door behind him, turning the key twice. He stops to listen for any noises in the house; then he counts his ammunition, glancing repeatedly toward the mountains.

Altogether he has only seven shots. He tosses the cartridges in his hand, smiles, and shakes his head as if to say that it does not matter. He slings his rifle over his shoulder and slowly walks across the clearing, heading toward the magazine.

Before entering the forest, he turns back to look at the empty house, the bench by the door, the steps to the porch, the everyday things dozing in wait. "Tonight . . . ," he murmurs, but then he smiles again, as the highest peaks gradually brighten.

21

Near the pass that opens into the ravine of the Polveriera, a slender spur juts out from the rockface and forms the ledge over which the brigands will arrive. The ledge is narrow and covered with gravel; you must be careful crossing it.

Barnabo stations himself on a peak above the pass, shielded by some boulders; he has come to face the enemy by himself. Completely hidden from sight, he commands the ledge from a distance and will be able to cut off the pass. This morning, when he left, he realized that he could die. But now he is already anticipating victory; he is certain that everything will turn out well. He could not have hoped to find a safer place. Lying in the sunlight, he feels time passing. They will come, by God, they will come.

From up there he can survey the entire ravine of the Polveriera and the great shadows cast on the gravel by the peaks; he again sees the Cima Alta lifting its savage walls beyond the blood-red Lastoni di Mezzo.

A light breeze arrives in the silent wait.

While the shadows move across the base of the dusty ravine, Barnabo lies motionless, his gun in his hands. He cannot be seen among the boulders on the low peak. His shotgun is aimed at the ledge. The brigands will pass by and he will be able to kill them.

It is strange that his heart does not pound. He is almost amazed that he feels so calm. Many things have changed. This is his great hour; it must not escape him. But now, in the vast silence, his gaze is fixed on the peaks that rise dizzily. His eyes ascend from one ledge to the other, up through the dark grooves in the reddish walls to the very top of the mountain, which does not seem real, so white is it against the deep blue sky.

A fly whirls by with a very light buzzing. The sunlight is momentarily obscured by a veil of mist. The southern wind also awakes again. The bad weather will return.

It was there, near the magazine (he can see it clearly from this height), that Barnabo had known fear one day; then, for years, he was ashamed of it. Yet in a little while, as he is well aware, the roar of his first shot will rip through the silence.

The great peaks meditate on what must happen. He will not die, not if he waits, if he feels absolutely sure of himself. He will rather be victorious: the brigands will plummet to the bottom, he will return to the village, the marvelous story will be told. The story, precisely, the story. He wants so much to be able to tell it to the other men. And it is all here: there's nothing else to say but I killed them by myself.

Then he will rejoin the foresters, who will throw a party for him and applaud his return. Later on, as the years pass, there will always be that barracks. How boring it will be at the foot of the valley, among the dusty roads.

A soft whistle becomes audible in the ravine. A little later you can hear some rocks rolling down the face of the mountain. The wind has suddenly stopped, leaving an immense silence. Then the sound of steps arrives from the far end of the ledge. He is not mistaken. At the corner of the spur a man's profile appears.

They advance slowly across the narrow, crumbling ledge. There are four of them in the bright sunshine. Another thirty seconds and Barnabo can fire. He will be able to cut them all down; there isn't the slightest cover, nor is there any way they can escape.

In the full light of the sun, Barnabo can distinguish them clearly; they are wearing old, torn clothes and carrying different kinds of rifles. They are thin, their faces sickly. The first must be about sixty; his shoulders are slightly stooped. They don't look bad.

These are the men who killed Del Colle and attacked the powder magazine. But so many memories have faded away. Perfectly calm, Barnabo is thinking of the old man after he rolls down the rocks, his head in the gravel, covered with blood. The bodies of his companions will be close by, one here, one there, like black, shapeless sacks.

He wants to be able to tell the story tomorrow, to glory in his victory. He really does not feel the need to take any revenge for himself. That moment of cowardice is now far away. Many years have passed; only now does he realize it. The rifle would frighten him now too, if he could be afraid.

He has quietly lifted the barrel of his shotgun. He finds the old man's head in the sight. They are not ten meters away; it would be a sure thing.

The old man stops and looks down, his right hand braced against the rocks. He turns to the others and says: "I don't see anyone." They too have stopped, and without thinking that Barnabo is observing them from the nearby peak, they notice that the magazine is deserted. No one is waiting for them; everything has been taken away.

So there is nothing left to do. Barnabo imagines the brigands returning down the mule trail toward Valfredda, hungry, not saying a word. Now he smiles: his finger touched the trigger; he felt the cold metal.

Silence. The buzzing of a fly, one of those mountain flies. The minutes do not pass during the wait for the shot.

This time it is not because of fear; something really remained in the past, something stayed behind while time rushed headlong. Barnabo smiles in the silence and lowers his gun; his hands relax. He feels happy, amid the peaks gilded by the sunlight. He notices the distant scent of the forest. The four brigands are now standing still; they seem to be waiting for something. Who knows whether they are the ones who killed Del Colle, or how they killed him. This is their last return. Tonight they will descend into Valfredda and disappear forever. And the peaks will remain more solitary than ever before. Barnabo will look after the house in the dark woods and think of the great victory that he had within his reach, but let pass by.

Everything will vanish in time—his stupid shame, the crow, the Bersaglio, Berton's departure—and every morning the sun will shine on the peaks once again. The fall will come, the snow, then the songs of spring.

A few meters away stand the four brigands, and he could kill them. Yet he lies motionless and thinks of all the useless pains they inflicted on his life. He thinks of the new house, now deserted, the tranquil meals, the light of the lamp, the days that follow all the other days; he even seems to hear the wind resounding through the trees.

The enemy turns back; slowly, just as they came, they cross the ledge. He lets them go. There is a great tranquility as night begins to fall.

Before nightfall the weather turns bad. The sky is filled with dense layers of clouds. Everything has remained quiet around the new house. You can hear the roof beams creaking. A hornet describes persistent circles over the grass in the clearing. Light breezes graze the trees.

A bird has begun to sing at the edge of the woods. The men are down at the village, playing boccie, walking through the square, calmly talking. Every so often there is laughter.

The clock strikes five. The peal of the bells echoes beyond the village and penetrates the forest, becoming more and more faint. Before the sound reaches the new house, it grows weary and must stop, tangled in the branches.

Barnabo has now returned. A short time ago, among the peaks, he broke a sort of enchantment. He remains completely alone. There are no longer any brigands or spirits; these things are gone. He walks at his usual pace and slowly crosses the clearing.

His boots resound on the porch. A spider has woven its web in a corner of the doorway; perhaps someone thought that Barnabo would not come back, that he might stay up there, near Del Colle and Darrìo, lying dead among the stones.

Having thrown open the windows to let in some light, Barnabo unloads his gun and returns it to the rack. Everything is in order. Nothing really happened.

A little later, as on the other evenings, he can perceive the reflection of the fire flickering against the windows. He is sitting near the flames. His face cannot be seen in the shadows.

The night of September 25th passes with weariness, a little wine, and many thoughts. After all, isn't it better this way? The fire continues to flicker, and the wood crackles. Perhaps it has begun to snow among the peaks. There should be a slow whirling between the black walls and, at the tip of a thin spire, Del Colle's cap, fastened with a nail. The snow will cover it again, forming a white crown.

Barnabo does not go to sleep. The night passes slowly. In a short while the dawn will brighten the horizon, and a new day will begin. Life continues to pass everywhere on the earth, uninterrupted.

He has lifted his head as if to listen. Is it his heartbeat or the sentry pacing outside the magazine? He is tired, a little sleepy; he can no longer remember. Then, as once before, in distant times, he takes his gun and approaches the door. Outside is the vast silence, and a pale light shines in the overcast sky. The mountains are hidden, but they feel close by. They stand motionless and solitary, immersed in the clouds.

(1933)

The Bewitched Bourgeois

One summer day Giuseppe Gaspari, a grain dealer who was forty-four years old, arrived at the mountain village where his wife and children were vacationing. Soon after he had gotten there and eaten lunch, almost everyone else went to sleep, so he set out by himself to take a walk.

He climbed a steep mule trail that ascended the mountain and turned around to observe the landscape. Despite the sun, he was disappointed. He had hoped that there might be a romantic valley with forests of pine and larch trees, surrounded by huge rock walls. This place, however, was at the foot of the Alps and enclosed within squat, truncated hills that looked desolate and grim. A hunter's paradise, thought Gaspari, regretting that he could never live, not even a few days, in one of those valleys, images of human happiness dominated by fantastic cliffs, where white, castellated hotels stand on the threshold of ancient forests fraught with legends. And with bitterness he considered how his entire life had been this way: he really had all he wanted, but everything always fell short of his desire, levelled to a sort of *via media* that satisfied his needs but never filled him with joy.

In the meantime he had gone up a good distance, and turning back, he was amazed to see that the village, hotel, and tennis court were already so small and faraway. He was about to resume his walk when beyond a low ridge he heard some voices.

Out of curiosity he left the mule trail, made his way through the thickets, and reached the top of the hill. There, hidden from the gaze of anyone who followed the beaten path, he discovered a wild gorge flanked by steep, crumbling slopes of red earth. Here and there stood a boulder, a bush, the dry remains of a tree. About fifty meters ahead, the gorge turned left, penetrating the side of the mountain. It was a viper's nest, scorched by the sun, strangely mysterious.

At that sight he was overcome with joy, but he did not have the faintest idea of why he reacted this way. The gorge was not particularly beautiful. Nevertheless, it had evoked in him some very strong feelings that he had not experienced for many years. It was as if he had recognized the crumbling hills, the deserted gully that gradually disappeared toward unexplored secrets, the gentle landslides whispering down the parched banks. Many years ago he had glimpsed them—many times—and what wonderful hours they had been. This was just like those magical lands of dreams and adventures, cherished at that age when everything is within the reach of hope.

But just below, behind an ingenuous hedge of stakes and blackberry bush, five young boys were talking together. They were bare-chested and wore strange berets, headbands, and belts to simulate exotic clothing or perhaps some sort of pirates' outfit. One had a popgun, the kind that shoots pellets. He was the oldest, about fourteen. The others were armed with bows made from hazel branches; for arrows they used small wooden hooks taken from the forks in twigs.

"Listen," said the oldest one. He was wearing three feathers in a headband. "It doesn't matter to me. . . . I won't worry about Sisto, you and Gino can take care of him—I hope. We only have to go slow, and you'll see, we'll take them by surprise."

Gaspari, listening to their talk, knew that they were playing cowboys-and-Indians: the palefaces were just up ahead, barricaded in an imaginary fort, and Sisto, the strongest and most awe-inspiring among them, was their leader. To take over the fort, the five boys were going to use a wooden plank about three meters long which they had brought with them just for this purpose. The plank could serve as a footbridge to cross a ditch or trench behind the enemy's stronghold (Gaspari really didn't know for sure). Two of the boys would advance straight across the base of the gorge, simulating a frontal attack, while the other three came up from the rear, making use of the plank.

Meanwhile one of them saw Gaspari standing at the top of the slope, that old, nearly bald man with the high forehead and bright, benevolent eyes. "Look over there," the boy said to his friends, who suddenly fell silent and stared distrustfully at the stranger.

"Hello," said Giuseppe in a very happy mood. "I was watching you. . . . And so: when do you begin the attack?"

The boys liked the idea that instead of scolding them, the strange man was practically encouraging. But they remained quiet, intimidated.

A ridiculous thought crossed Giuseppe's mind. He jumped down the side of the gorge, his feet sinking into the gravel that slid beneath him, and bounded toward the boys, who all stood up. Then he asked them:

"Do you want me to be on your side? I can carry the board, it's too heavy for you."

The boys smiled a little. What did he want, this stranger they had never encountered in the village? Yet seeing his genial face, they started to consider him with greater indulgence.

"Sisto is over there," the youngest boy told him to see if he would be frightened.

"Is Sisto so terrible?"

"He always wins," the boy answered. "He sticks his fingers in your face; it's like he wants to dig out your eyes. He's nasty . . ."

"Nasty? You'll see, we'll give him some of his own medicine!" said Gaspari, amused.

And so they set off. Gaspari, helped by another boy, lifted the plank. It weighed much more than he had anticipated. Then they headed for the nearest side of the gorge, making their way through the boulders at the base. The children looked at him with astonishment. It was strange that he didn't show the slightest trace of patronizing them, as the other adults did when they condescended to play. He really seemed to take it seriously.

When they reached the foot of the slope, they stopped and crouched down behind some rocks, slowly sticking out their heads to observe. Gaspari followed their example and stretched out in the gravel, not worrying about his clothes.

Then he saw the rest of the gorge, which was even more striking and wild than he had imagined. Conical mounds of red earth that appeared very fragile rose all around, densely crowded together like the spires of a dilapidated cathedral. They had a vague, unsettling appearance, as if they had remained there for centuries, immobile, waiting for someone. And on the top of the tallest mound, which stood at the highest point of the gorge, he could see a sort of low stone wall with three heads sticking out above it.

"Look up there," whispered one of the boys. "Do you see them?"

He nodded that he did, but he was confused. The distance was actually not that great. All the same, for a few moments he asked himself how they would manage to get up there, on that remote cliff suspended over the chasm. Would they reach it before nightfall? No sooner had he asked this question than he forgot it. What was he thinking of? It was only a matter of a hundred or so meters!

Two of the boys stopped to wait. They would move on only at the right moment. The others, with Gaspari, clambered up the slope to reach the rim of the gorge, careful to avoid being seen.

"Go slow, don't move any stones," Gaspari recommended in a low voice, more anxious than the others about the outcome of the assault. "Buck up now, we'll be there in a little while."

They reached the top of the slope and descended a few meters into an adjoining valley that was rather shallow. From here they resumed their trek, holding the plank in front of them.

The plan had been well calculated. When they came out of the valley, the cowboys' fort appeared just below, about ten meters away. Now they had to climb down into the bushes and throw the plank across a narrow ditch. The enemy was calmly sitting down, and Sisto stood out among them. He wore a coonskin cap, and a yellowish paper mask, intentionally frightening, hid half his face. (Meanwhile a cloud had lowered over them, the sun vanished, and the gorge turned a leaden color.)

"Here we are," whispered Gaspari. "I'm going on with the board."

He lifted the plank and slowly edged his way down into the black-berry bushes, followed by the others. If the cowboys didn't notice them, they would manage to reach their goal.

But here Gaspari stopped, as if absorbed (the cloud had still not budged; from afar he heard a mournful shout that sounded like his name). "What a strange turn of events," he thought. "Only two hours ago I was at the hotel with my wife and children, sitting at the table; now here I am in this unexplored land, thousands of kilometers away, fighting with some Indians."

Gaspari looked around. The gorge adapted to children's games, the mediocre truncated hills, the path that ascended the mountain, the hotel, the red tennis court had all vanished. Beneath him he saw im-mense cliffs, different from anything he could remember, endlessly precipitating toward seas of forests. Farther on was the shimmering glare of the deserts and farther still the gleam of other lights, other confused signs denoting the mystery of the world. And here, in front of him, on the edge of a cliff, stood an ominous castle; it was perched on perilously steep rock walls, and its battlements were crowned with skulls that were bleached by the sun and seemed to laugh. This was the land of curses and myths, the unbroken solitude, the ultimate truth granted to our dreams!

A half-closed wooden door (which did not exist) was covered with sinister marks. It groaned every time the wind blew. Gaspari was now very close, perhaps two meters away. He started to lift the plank slowly so as to let it fall on the other side of the ditch.

"Ambushed!" Sisto shouted at that very instant, having spotted the attack, and he leaped to his feet, laughing, armed with a huge bow. When he noticed Gaspari, he stopped for a moment, perplexed. Then he pulled one of those wooden hooks from his pocket, fitted the in-nocuous dart in the bowstring, and took aim.

Yet the door with the obscure signs (which did not exist) creaked on its hinges, and Gaspari saw a sorcerer appear, a hellish figure en-crusted with leprosy. He saw him stand erect, very tall, saw his vacant, soulless glances and a bow in his hand, drawn back with an awful force. Gaspari then let the plank go and retreated in fear. But the other had already taken his shot.

Struck in the chest, Gaspari fell among the bushes.

He returned to the hotel after nightfall. He was exhausted. He sank to a bench near the main entrance. People came and went, someone said hello to him, others did not recognize him because it was already dark.

Yet he was intensely withdrawn into himself and did not pay any attention to the people. And no one who had passed by noticed that an arrow was driven into the middle of his chest. The shaft, turned to perfection and apparently made of a dark, very hard wood, rose about thirty-five centimeters from his shirt, at the center of a blood stain. Gaspari stared at it with a horror that was rather moderate because mixed with a curious joy. He had tried to pull out the arrow, but it hurt him too much: the barbed point must have been biting into his flesh. And every so often blood gurgled from the wound. He felt sweat dripping down his chest and belly, soaking the folds of his shirt.

It was thus that Giuseppe Gaspari's hour had arrived, with a magnificence that was at once poetic and cruel. He was probably near death, he thought. And yet how sweet was his revenge against life, people, conversations, faces, the mediocrity that had always surrounded him. And how triumphant! Of course he was not now returning from that little valley a few minutes away from the Hotel Corona. He had come back from a very remote land set apart from human irreverence, the pure kingdom of sorcerers; and to get there, the others (not he) needed to cross oceans and travel great distances through inhospitable solitudes, struggling against the hostility of nature and the weakness of man, yet even then it could not be said that they had arrived. He, however . . .

He was the man in his forties who played with children, taking the game as seriously as they did. The difference was that there is a kind of angelic lightness in children, whereas he played with a ponderous, rabid faith over which he had brooded for who knows how many years without being aware of it. His faith was so strong that it made everything come true—the gorge, the Indians, the blood. He had entered a world that was no longer the one he recalled from fairy tales, beyond the boundary that after a certain age cannot be crossed with impunity. He had said "Open" to a secret door, almost believing that he was joking, but the door had really opened. He had said "Indians," and there were Indians. The arrow in the game had become a real arrow, which was now killing him.

So he had paid his ransom, the price for his arduous enchantment; he had passed the point of no return. Yet he consoled himself with his revenge. His wife, his children, his friends at the hotel would all be expecting him at dinner, at the nightly bridge game. The pastina in brodo, the boiled beef, the news broadcast—it was enough to make you laugh. They were expecting him, the man who had just emerged from the dark recesses of the world!

"Beppino," called his wife. She was standing on the terrace overlooking the spot where the tables had been set up al fresco. "What are you doing, sitting over there? And where have you been? Still in those white socks? Aren't you going to change? Don't you know it's past eight o'clock? We're starving. . ."

". . . amen . . ." Did Gaspari hear that voice? Or was he already far away? He made a vague gesture with his right hand, as if to say that they should leave him alone, they could go on without him, he didn't give a damn. He even smiled. His face wore an expression of bitter gladness, although his breathing was shallow.

"Come now, Beppino," shouted the wife. "Do you want to keep us waiting? What's wrong with you? Why don't you answer? Does anyone know why he isn't answering?"

He lowered his head as if to say yes, but did not raise it again. He was finally a real man, not a wretch. A hero, not a worm, not to be confused with the others, he was above them now. And alone. His head hung on his chest, as happens with the dead, and a slight smile was frozen on his lips, signifying his contempt. I have beaten you, miserable world, you couldn't hold me back.

(1948)

Personal
Escort

Outside the gate, a score of meters beyond the old customs house, someone is waiting for me.

I saw him for the first time many years ago, when I was a child. To amuse myself I had climbed the ancient walls of the city where I lived, and I saw a man standing in an outer field. He was dressed in gray, and he stared at me with interest. Since he was at least four hundred meters away, I could not tell whether he was young or old, ugly or handsome, poor or wealthy. He was carrying a walking stick, so he might have been taking a stroll when he stopped to look at me. To climb the walls at that point, you had to scale a very steep rampart that had been severely eroded. Hence I thought that the stranger was looking at me with a certain admiration and, flattered, I waved at him to say hello. He lifted his stick and shook it weakly, as if to signify a vague complicity between us: it made a curious impression on me. Not long after, I saw a caravan of gypsies in those fields on the outskirts, so I suspected that he was a gypsy, one who was perhaps planning to kidnap me. Nevertheless, the hour was so pleasant and serene, the afternoon sun so warm (even if rather dim), and the man's appearance so inoffensive that my fear could not last long. Yet the banal dread of kidnapping gave way to a thought that was new and disquieting for me, and that I will never be able to explain: it was as if I had discovered that apart from family, school, and friends, another life was waiting for me, until now unforeseen, but still mine, a mysterious life which I had entered unlawfully.

But this was a brief thought. Within a few minutes I was descending the walls. And I probably would have never remembered that afternoon if three years later, having ridden my bicycle to the city limits, I did not notice a man in a field who seemed to be staring at me intensely: he was in every way similar to the one I had seen from the walls, with the same calm expression, the same walking stick. This could be considered an ordinary coincidence. At a distance of three years how could my memory be so precise? And what of the countless men who may have strolled through that field, dressed almost identically, having the same build, and carrying walking sticks? And yet instantly I was certain that it was the same man, and relying on my bicycle for a quick getaway if worst came to worst, I drew closer to have a better look. But either because I did not take the right road, or because in that brief interval he had moved away, or because I was confused, I reached the field and saw, not one, but five individuals, none of whom looked at me, none of whom resembled the man I sought.

All the same, the encounter aroused obscure apprehensions within me. And I suspected that I too had embarked on one of those extraordinary adventures, of a magical character, that I had read about in books. From time to time, men were in fact called by fate to take part in them, but these summons grew more and more rare as the years gradually passed.

Yet the adventure did not occur. I went on with my usual life and the thought of the man standing in the field wound up leaving me. I had now grown up, and such things seemed nothing more than stupid childish fantasies.

The situation remained this way for a decade. Then I happened to visit a foreign city for a brief period. There, as I was driving in a car one night along a suburban street, I noticed beyond the last houses, in a smooth, tranquil field, an individual who was looking at me, signalling with a walking stick.

Now it is useless to ask me how I knew that he was looking at me and not someone else with so many people and cars passing by. Nor can I say how I knew that it was the same man from that distant day, that spy from an unknown realm who had pursued me around the world and was now waiting for me at the gates of the city. It was undoubtedly he.

From then on I saw him many times. No matter what city I chose, as soon as I left the inhabited area, or climbed the campanile to gaze out over the countryside, I saw him. And for some time, whenever I thought about it, I was afraid: that man was obviously following me, besieging me; perhaps at night he would enter the city, walk down the deserted streets, reach my house, surprise me in my sleep, and carry out his dark purposes. And how could I defend myself? The few times that I had boldly decided to confront him, something always happened to prevent the encounter: he suddenly disappeared, or other people arrived to create confusion, or I was bewildered.

What did he want from me? If I managed to get to him—I used to say to myself—he would probably turn out to be some vagrant who just happened to be there, and my curiosity would astonish him. Yet not even this was enough to calm me down. So I avoided the outskirts to spare myself the anxiety of seeing the threatening apparition. And I thought that perhaps if he did not see me anymore, he would get bored and move far away. Would the persecution last my entire life?

But many years have passed, I am now an old man, and he is still down there, beyond the walls of any city where I choose to live. And lately I have had more than one glimpse of him. Although I may have been lost in the crowd that piled into a bus, or hidden behind a curtain, or protected by the darkness, his placid stare was fixed on me, not anyone else.

My reader may feel compelled to object: when I am in the country or at sea, where does he wait for me? But this is a ridiculous difficulty. If I stay in the country, he appears in the vicinity, although always at a certain distance, and for a man like him who loves the fields, there is only the problem of choosing one among so many. If, on the other hand, I travel by sea, he always knows the next port of call; as the ship approaches land, I can be certain that he has gotten there ahead of me and is calmly strolling along the dock.

I am aware of all this, yet now my apprehension has ended. I am no longer afraid of him. And I still don't know what he wants from me, why he makes such a great effort to follow me, or where he comes from (since he is certainly not a creature of this world). In fact, I recently have succeeded, not in understanding—since this story is forever wrapped in mystery—but in suspecting something about his real intentions. I am persuaded, that is to say, that the stranger does not want to hurt me, does not desire to persecute me, and does not think of assaulting me at night when I am asleep. He is content to wait. He follows me from city to city and stays in the background, exposed to the wind and rain so as not to annoy me, certain that one day I will finally have to stop. It may be that after many years—although I don't know whether this is his hope—I shall enter a city, or village, for the last time; I mean that this city will signify the conclusion to my journey and I will never be able to leave it (at least not in the usual sense of the word). Only then will he decide. Only then will he pass through the gate, proceed along the streets at a tranquil pace, arrive at my house, and knock on the door with his walking stick.

I am not afraid of him anymore. Actually, as the days pass, I feel rather grateful for him. The years devour themselves, my face ages, the house where I lived as a child has disappeared, the friends who have given me so many beautiful memories are gradually dying, every spring finds me increasingly alone, fewer and fewer people care for me, my hopes dwindle away. But he waits for me with infinite patience. Little by little my life will become utterly desolate, but I am certain that he will be the only one who remains faithful to me, standing in a field on the outskirts, leaning on his stick. Only he, in the end, will not desert me; only he will be near in the most difficult hour of my life. Why, then, should I hate him? Why hope that he will leave?

How things have changed since that day when I climbed the walls. Would you believe me if I say that sometimes I almost hurry to meet him, come what may, that I am impatient to see his face at last, to know what message he will draw from a pocket of his gray suit and hand me with a smile?

(1948)

An
Interrupted
Story

I would like to finish an old story left interrupted many years ago. I found it by chance in a drawer. For the first time in my life, I happened to read a piece that I did not remember writing, and I was amazed. There are three and a half pages in my normal handwriting. They have yellowed a bit, it pains me to say, and in fact they are coated with a light patina of dissolution, weariness, and death, even though scarcely ten years have passed.

For ten years, then, the unfinished story has waited, preserving its burden of emotion, the joy and perhaps the tears that had made it grow within me. (Or did it exhaust itself somehow, without my awareness, and no longer obeying my intention, develop randomly, but without words, compelled by some senseless caprice?) With a sad shudder, I realized that I no longer recalled the continuation I had imagined. How did I want it to end? I felt as if someone else had invented it, a different man, a stranger. And he had disappeared forever.

Yet in the fragment I recognized one of the landscapes that I am fond of, a rather romantic place where even now I like to travel. The pages contained a description of a huge house, a sort of roadside inn, which stood among several rustic dwellings in a solitary valley; on every side rose cliffs of red earth, farther above was pasture, and higher still the dark woods. The mountains loomed in the distance with their impenetrable secrets. At the beginning of the story, some hunters had gathered in the ground-floor room, and they were sitting in front of glasses of wine. They were talking somewhat allusively about a strange, troubling incident that had happened, or was happening, or could happen (it is impossible to tell from the unfinished piece). Outside the summer afternoon reigned, with its intense, silent sunlight full of anticipation. The road ran by the house, white with dust, absolutely deserted as far as the eye could see. At this point my reader may be moved to interject (not without irony): And were there not brigands in the mountains? There were, probably. And spirits too? Spirits and ghosts that descend into the valley at night to frighten travellers? Precisely, my friend, spirits and ghosts. These things were not explicitly mentioned in the piece, but we cannot discount the possibility that they might have appeared later on.

The third page relates that in the immense quiet, a woman's rich song issued from a window in the house. Her name is mentioned: Marietta. But wait: now I remember her! She was young, sweet, kind. As she tidied up the room, Marietta sang, abandoning herself to confused presentiments of love. I recall her vividly. Yet it is here that the story breaks off.

So the plot had still not taken shape. There was only a heavy atmosphere of suspense and mystery, the kind of vague foreboding that hangs over certain days. And now that I think of it, something else occurs to me: I remember that somebody was going to come down the road, a man on horseback carrying news. He was a very significant person, one of those popularly called messengers of fate. At his arrival a great, poetic event would unfold. Exactly what was it? I don't remember.

I am really unable to recall what the rider's appearance might have meant. And yet today I would like to write on and finish the story; I think it would make me feel younger. Here I am, then, in the dog days, on a deserted road at the base of the valley. I approach the house. I see an old man sitting by the door; I could swear that he wasn't there ten years ago. "Good day," I say. He raises his eyes and returns the greeting.

"How is it going?" I ask. "Still strong? Are the hunters still inside?"

"The hunters?" he says, amazed. "What hunters?"

The house is quiet, too quiet. There is no sound of talking or glasses in the ground-floor room. I notice that the girl's song is missing.

"And Marietta?" I ask the old man. "Is she here at least?"

This time the old man shows that he understands. He turns his head to the door and shouts twice: "Marietta!" She appears a little later.

She looks out on the road and says hello, rather nonchalantly. What a splendid woman she has become. Her smiling red lips wear a vivid, brazen expression. But how different she is from then. I must confess that I am intimidated by her.

"Excuse me, Miss," I say to her (it is impossible for me to be familiar with her), "did that man on horseback arrive? What news did he bring?"

"A man on horseback? I really don't know, Sir." She smiles invitingly. "I don't know any riders, so I really don't know."

I look at her. Her eyes are deep; they contain her innermost thoughts.

"He should have come from down there," I explain, pointing to the road. "He was supposed to be carrying news. Don't you remember?"

"I really wouldn't know, Sir. I'm sorry . . ."

Then I think: how stupid I am; it is only natural for her not to know. I left everything hanging in the air at a crucial moment. No one but me can know about that rider; without me he could not arrive. I must be the one to summon him.

"Forgive me," I say to Marietta. "But tell me: do you sing anymore? Do you still enjoy singing sometimes?"

She laughs, diverted by the idea, parting her beautiful lips. "Yes, sometimes I do, if I'm in the mood . . ."

"Listen," I insist, "I have a favor to ask you. Please don't think I am joking. Would you go to your room a moment, open the window, and sing a little?"

"Sing? Just like that, by myself? Right now?"

"Right now. I ask you sincerely."

"And what shall I sing?"

"A song, what do I know? Whatever you like, any song."

"Well, if there is really nothing else you'd like better!" She goes inside the house, and I hear her steps on the stairs.

The old landscape is intact. The quiet summer sunlight is the same as it was that day, ten years ago. And the atmosphere seems just as mysterious and disquieting. Marietta has now begun to sing, as in the last lines of the interrupted manuscript. The beautiful Marietta will sing and at the foot of the road the rider will automatically appear, bearing his weight of destiny. Everything will be set in motion again, and after ten years the story will resume, as if I had not left it unfinished so long ago.

Marietta's window opened. She looked out and saw that I was not smiling. Then she went back inside. And in the silence she lifted her voice.

I listened, motionless, and my heart grew troubled. What had happened? Was Marietta the woman who was singing? Did she possess this impure voice, clouded with unconfessed memories? This voice had known so many things, so many pitiful joys and fallen illusions, so many lies. It was overburdened with shameful sorrows, and it painfully labored to contain them all. The woman who had been Marietta was singing, abandoning herself with much cruelty to confused regrets of love. I listened to her. And I remembered everything.

You were a rose when I saw you that first time, many years ago, and this story began. What happened? You were a pure, graceful flower, uncontaminated. You smiled at the world like a little fountain, and spring dreams fluttered lightly about you, caressing your eyes and lips. The sweet enchantment of youth had still not betrayed you. My God, what has happened? You used to sing like the cardinals at dawn, timidly turned toward the unknown happiness that was there waiting for you. Nothing of the sad world, not the slightest shadow, had fallen over you. And everything, even the most incredible tales, were possible that day, that brief day; it was beneath your window that the famous rider would have stopped.

You were a little flower, but now as I hear you again, I realize that ten years have passed. The old man by the door sways his head, accompanying the desolate song; he even smiles with foolish pleasure. I see the cliffs all around, the pastures, the woods, the infinite mountains. Icy shadows. Who remembers anything about the brigands? Who has heard any more talk of spirits? The road is deserted, no one is approaching, there is no echo of a distant gallop, and it is pointless to wait. The air, yes, it still carries a dark, profound anticipation. But for something else, at this point, something very different. Who knows what: perhaps the rider has already passed through, perhaps he arrived after a very long journey and set out again, in the opposite direction, without even stopping. Of course we shall never see him again. The old story died within me, but I did not notice it. Only a fragment remains, and it is too late to start over.

(1948)

The
Gnawing
Worm

Today I was standing at the window when I saw a man pass by. He was about my age, medium height, dark hair, moustache, properly dressed. Since he happened to look up, he saw me, then waved, smiling, and shouted: "Hello Andrea!"

Who was he? His face wasn't new to me, but I couldn't give it a name. Was he a friend from school or the service? To avoid seeming rude, I too said hello. Then he nodded allusively, as if to say: "Hey, do you remember the good old days?" Embarrassed, I moved away from the window.

I ran into him on the street. He embraced me. "The other day I recognized you immediately! I said to myself: that's Andrea Filari! . . .

But you . . . tell me the truth . . . it was strange that you didn't recognize me."

"Well . . . you understand," I said, "you must forgive me . . .
after so many years. . . I have such a wretched memory. . ."

His face was smooth and oval-shaped, his eyes dark brown, liquid, very warm. "But I'm Molla, Egidio Molla! We were in high
school together. . . how can you not remember? We were like brothers . . . then my family moved to Rimini . . . and later you wrote me
all those letters, a stack about this high, I still have them."

"Forgive me," I repeated, although I absolutely could not remember, "but this was so long ago. Yet now that I give it some
thought. . . yes, now I remember. So tell me: what kind of work do
you do?"

We talked about ourselves. I am an antique dealer, in my father's
old business, married, no children. He said that he is a bachelor, a pub-
licist by profession, head of public relations for a huge chemical cor-
poration. He also writes for magazines. On the whole, however, I had
the feeling that things were not going well for him. Then there were
the usual promises to get together. I gave him my home telephone
number, he the number of the boarding house where he was living.
"How glad I am to see you again, old Andrea! I don't know why, but
I have a sort of premonition that our meeting like this will bring me
some luck." I, on the other hand, tried to cut it short. I felt uneasy. It's
so strange: no matter how hard I try, no matter how carefully I sift
through my high school memories, I cannot come up with the slightest trace of Egidio Molla.

When it started raining this afternoon, I hurried to close the windows,
and whom did I see down in the street? It was Molla, standing in the
downpour, working on a bicycle, probably a tire or the chain. This
street is lined with small townhouses, and there really isn't any place
where he could get out of the rain. I didn't make a sound, but he saw
me at once. He laughed and made a gesture of hopelessness, as if to
say: "This takes more patience than I have!"

What could I do? Leave him there to drown? I went down to the
door and invited him inside. He was already soaked to the bone. I introduced him to my wife. He seemed shy, all smiles and compli-

ments. His movements were lethargic. Every so often he paused and fell silent, staring at me with those oppressive, slanted eyes.

"It will revive, it will, you'll see," he suddenly murmured, as if he were revealing to me some marvelous news that had not yet been released to the public.

"What do you mean?"

"Why, our old friendship, no?"

What nerve he had to show this affection to me, especially since I was another man: I found it rather impudent. "Perhaps," I answered icily. "In the meantime, as long as it is raining, come and see my house."

I must confess that I have a weakness for my house. All antique furniture, several canvases by old masters. And then there is the library, which would impress anyone: it is a large room completely filled with volumes (there must be more than twenty thousand). They are works of history for the most part, particularly French history from the Revolution to the present. Molla—but he insists that I call him simply Egidio—was all admiration.

"It's fantastic, fantastic . . . Ah, for me this would be a gold mine—paradise. I'm writing a book, you know, I've been working on it for two years now. It's about Napoleon's marshals and I see that you have everything here . . . texts I couldn't find anywhere. Tell me, Andrea, would you mind—but no, it would be such a nuisance to you."

"What?" I asked without enthusiasm.

"No, no, God forbid that I should be a bother to friends, to a true friend!"

"Please, tell me."

"Well, I was thinking whether you might permit me to come some time to consult certain books . . . I wouldn't disturb you . . . I won't make any noise . . . I'll just sit myself in a corner."

He didn't want to waste any time. In fact, he showed up the next day. It was quarter to nine. I still hadn't left. He came in on tiptoe, as if to pass by unnoticed. He brought me a package. "I thought they might give you pleasure. . . . I bet you don't have this work. . . . They are books that belonged to my grandfather." I opened it. Pleasure indeed:

it was one of the most common editions of Taine, such as you can buy for a pittance at the outdoor stalls.

Yet because of my usual cowardice I pretended to be enthusiastic. I thanked him and invited him to sit at my desk. He protested. "No, no. This is your place . . . absolutely not. I could never forgive myself for it. Look: I'll just settle down with my papers at that small table in the corner. And you go about your business as if I didn't exist."

When I returned from the shop at one, I asked my wife: "Is he still in the library?"

"I believe so. . . . The poor fellow, he isn't the slightest trouble."

We set the table. The clatter of the dishes certainly reached as far as the library.

"But when does he eat?" asked my wife.

"What do I know?"

During the meal we listened carefully to see if there was any sign of life from the library. It is such a nuisance to know that while you are eating, someone in the next room is going hungry.

For four days he remained shut up in the library from nine in the morning till late afternoon without a break. Today my wife—might she never have done it—invited him to stop for lunch.

"No, no, Signora," he replied, "it's out of the question, absolutely out of the question . . . and then I never eat lunch. . . . No, that would be the last straw . . . here I am disturbing you every day. Andrea is so good . . . friendship is such a sacred thing, but it also is rather delicate. There are certain limits . . ."

Maria naturally found herself compelled to insist. He held fast, staring at her with his watery eyes. Maria kept insisting: he might accept her invitation if for no other reason but to please her. At this Egidio finally yielded, as if it were a sacrifice for him. And at lunch he ate hardly two mouthfuls.

Since Egidio has been working in the library during the evenings as well, we wound up entertaining him at supper. His appetite has now returned. You might even say that he stuffs himself. And he keeps on telling my wife: "You are a sorceress, you could tempt a saint, you know how to spiritualize, to transform into poetry the sad necessity of nourishment." Egidio, in fact, often indulges in this sort of weak, effusive claptrap.

Last night, around two o'clock, I thought I heard a rustling noise in the library. Rats? I got out of bed to see. It was he, Egidio, still there among the books. "Don't you ever go home? Forgive me, but you understand, I must go down to open the gate for you, and frankly, I'm sleepy."

"Did I wake you?" he said, dismayed. "You can't imagine how sorry I am. . . . I was thinking of spending the night here, I'm used to it. Go on, Andrea, go back to bed. I don't want you to catch cold on my account."

He led me back to the room (Maria sleeps in another) like a mother with her child. Then he jokingly tucked me in and sat on the edge of the bed, chattering away.

"I envy you for being able to sleep so easily. . . . I would too, if I were in your shoes. . . . If only you felt my bed at the boarding house. This is what I call a bed. . . . Two people could fit in here and there would still be room to move around, look how comfortable it is (in fun he lay down beside me, he on top of the covers, me beneath them) . . . ah, what bliss! . . . How lucky you are . . . how I—" He continued his game by closing his eyes and pretending to snore.

But was he pretending? It seemed too real. I shook him. "Egidio, Egidio!" He didn't budge. "Egidio, wake up!" Nothing. Except for his snoring. He was sleeping like a rock.

He spent the night in my bed. I was on the couch in the wardrobe. I couldn't stay next to him, it would have been too much for me. And this morning he woke me up. I saw him kneeling at my side, on the brink of tears: "Andrea, Andrea, I'm leaving! I can't stay here any longer. . . . Forgive me, if you can . . . what I've done is horrible . . . rob you of your bed! You see, I suddenly felt sick, I thought you would understand, but I know this isn't any excuse. . . . A man not as good as you might even think I wanted to exploit those books I gave you . . . another man would have thrown me out of the bed . . . and then—then, Andrea, let me make a complete confession. . . . I can no longer set foot in a house where the maid shows me no respect."

"Who? Carolina?"

"Yes, precisely . . . with my own ears I heard her while she was talking to another servant. She said: *that damned freeloader will leave sooner or later!* Those were her very words. . . . Do you see how poverty can stain even the purest sentiment of friendship?" He was sobbing. And as the tears streamed down his cheeks, he flashed those grave, unctuous looks.

He stayed, we begged him so much to stay. He stayed, but with a slightly offended air. To the old and faithful Carolina (after twelve years) we gave a week's notice. Egidio eats with us day and night. And then he goes to sleep in my bed. He is now the boss. But he is always timid, reserved, attentive. When my wife and I are alone, for some reason we avoid talking about him. Are we ashamed? Or afraid of being sincere? Or is there something between Maria and him?

Today Egidio gave me a long, pathetic speech. He wants to repay his debts in some way. He asked me to take him to work in the shop: he says he will keep the books, receive customers, do the cleaning, anything as long as he can be useful.

He has worked in the shop for two weeks. He says he is taking an inventory of the merchandise. He maintains that it is indispensable. Very scrupulous, he has put the shop above everything else and every day he assigns himself an enormous task. Is he useful to me? On the contrary. But I know how certain things turn out. So, to avoid any lawsuits in the future, I wanted to give him a small salary. He became indignant: "Am I or am I not your best friend? Helping you is my first obligation." Later, although he won't admit it, he started acting like a victim who sacrifices himself for the good of others.

I am going to murder him. It's the only thing to do. Tonight. I'll shoot him in his sleep and then make it look like a suicide.

Around three o'clock, a pistol in my hand, I entered his room, the one that had been mine until a few weeks ago. The blinds were open, and I could see well enough by the glare of the streetlights. It must have taken me a quarter of an hour to reach the bed. I advanced barefoot, invaded by an inexpressible joy. As usual he was snoring like an animal. When I got to the bed, I raised the revolver to his temple. At that precise moment—was he only pretending to be asleep? had he sensed my presence in the room?—Egidio lifted a hand and put his palm to the barrel, as if to stop the bullet. I can't say whether it was an accident or not, but the gun went off.

I turned on the light. The entire bed was stained with blood. Egidio's left palm was perforated. "Oh Andrea, why, why? . . . What did I do to you? We were like two brothers . . . brothers . . . and you want to kill me. . . . Why, Andrea? Why have you done this?" And he wept desperately.

Meanwhile Maria had arrived, terrorized. "It's nothing, Signora," said Egidio, sitting up in bed, patting the wound with a handkerchief. "Don't be frightened . . . it was an accident. Please, Signora, don't look at me like that. . . . You should know me by now. . . . You mustn't be afraid. . . . I won't talk, I won't, I swear to you . . . I will carry this secret to the grave. . . . That would be the last straw, after all your kind gestures to denounce you to the police!"

I am his slave now. The house is his. He is the one who orders the meals. He is the one who does the family's accounts. Maria understands and keeps quiet. A painter is redoing the name on the sign of my antique shop. "Filari" used to be painted there. Now you can read "Filari and Molla."

This is as it should be. Since yesterday Egidio has been my partner. The papers were drawn up by a lawyer. The arrangement is fifty-fifty. And he hasn't put in a penny. He is forever timid, considerate, modest, docile. When we are alone, his slimy glances shift from my eyes to the scar on his hand, from the scar to my eyes. And he smiles pleasantly at me, like someone who knows how to forgive.

(1954)

The
Time
Machine

The first great installation to slow down time was built near Grosseto, in Mariscano. In fact, the inventor, the famous Aldo Cristofari, was a native of Grosseto. This Cristofari, a professor at the University of Pisa, had been interested in the problem for at least twenty years and had conducted marvelous experiments in his laboratory, especially on the germination of legumes. In the academic world, however, he was thought a visionary. Until, under the aegis of his supporter, the financier Alfredo Lopez, the society for the construction of Diacosia was created. From then on Aldo Cristofari was regarded as a genius, a benefactor to humanity.

His invention consisted of a special electrostatic field called "Field C," within which natural phenomena required an abnormally longer period of time to complete their life cycles. In the first decisive experiments, this delay did not exceed five or six units per thousand; in practice, that is to say, it was almost unnoticeable. Yet once Cristofari had discovered the principle, he made very rapid progress. With the installation at Mariscano the rate of retardation was increased to nearly half. This meant that an organism with an average life span of ten years could be inserted in Field C and reach an age of twenty.

The installation was built in a hilly zone, and it was not effective beyond a range of 800 meters. In a circle with a diameter of one and a half kilometers, animals and plants would grow and age half as quickly as those on the rest of the earth. Man could now hope to live for two centuries. And so—from the Greek for two hundred—the name Diacosia was chosen.

The zone was practically uninhabited. The few peasants who lived there were given the choice of staying or relocating with a sizeable settlement. They preferred to clear out. The area was entirely enclosed within an insurmountable fence. There was only one entrance, and it was carefully guarded. In a short time there rose immense skyscrapers, a gigantic nursing home (for terminally ill patients who desired to prolong the little life they had left), movie houses, and theaters, all amid a forest of fantastic mansions. And in the middle, at a height of forty meters, stood a circular antenna similar to those used for radar; this constituted the center of Field C. The power plant was completely underground.

Once the installation was finished, the entire world was informed that within three months the city would open its doors. To gain admission, and above all to reside there, cost an enormous sum. All the same, thousands of people from every corner of the globe were tempted. The subscriptions quickly exhausted the available housing. But then the fear began, and the flow of applicants was slower than anticipated.

What was there to fear? First of all, anyone who had settled in the city for any appreciable length of time could not leave without injury. Imagine an organism accustomed to the new, slower pace of physical existence. Suddenly transplant it from Field C to an area where life moves twice as fast; the function of every organ would have to accelerate immediately. And if it is easy for a runner to slow down, it is not so easy for someone moving slowly to bolt into a mad dash. The violent disequilibrium could have harmful or simply fatal consequences.

As a result, anyone who was born in the city was strictly forbidden to leave it. It was only logical to expect that an organism created in that slower speed could not be shifted to an environment that ran, we might say, in double time without risking destruction. In anticipation of this problem, special booths for acceleration and retardation were to be constructed on the perimeter of Field C so that anyone who left or entered it might gradually acclimate himself to the new pace and avoid the trauma of an abrupt change (they were similar to decompression chambers for deep-sea divers). But these booths were delicate devices, still in the planning stage. They would not be in service for many years.

In short, the citizens of Diacosia would live much longer than other men and women, but in exile. They were forced to give up their country, old friends, travel. They could no longer have a variety of lovers and acquaintances. It was as if they had been sentenced to life imprisonment, although they enjoyed every imaginable luxury and convenience.

But there was more. The danger posed by an escape could also be caused by any damage to the installation. It is true that there were two generators in the power plant, and that if one stopped, the other began to operate automatically. But what if both malfunctioned? What if there was a blackout? What if a cyclone or lightning struck the antenna? What if there was a war, or some outrage?

Diacosia was inaugurated at a celebration for its first group of citizens, who numbered 11,365. For the most part, they were people over fifty. Cristofari, who did not intend to settle in the city, was absent. He was represented by one Stoermer, a Swiss who was the director of the installation. There was a simple ceremony.

At the foot of the transmitting antenna that rose in the public garden, precisely at noon, Stoermer announced that from that moment on in Diacosia men and women would age exactly one-half as slowly as before. The antenna emitted a very soft hum, which was, moreover, pleasing to the ear. In the beginning, no one noticed the altered conditions. Only toward evening did some people feel a kind of lethargy, as if they were being held back. Very soon they started to talk, walk, chew with their usual composure. The tension of life slackened. Everything required greater effort.

About one month later, in *Technical Monthly*, a magazine based in Buffalo, the Nobel laureate Edwin Mediner published an article that proved to be the death knell for Diacosia. Mediner maintained that Cristofari's installation carried a grave threat. Time—we here present a synthesis of his argument in plain words—tends to rush headlong, and if it does not encounter the resistance of any matter, it will assume a progressively accelerated pace, with a tendency to increase to infinity. Thus any retardation of the flow of time requires immense effort, while it is nothing at all to augment its speed—just as in a river it is difficult to go against the current, but easy to follow it. From this observation Mediner formulated the following law: If one wishes to slow down natural phenomena, the necessary energy is directly proportional to the square of the retardation to be obtained; if one wishes to speed them up, on the other hand, the acceleration is directly proportional to the cube of the necessary energy. For example, ten units of energy are enough to achieve an acceleration of one thousand units; but the same ten units of energy applied to achieve the opposite purpose hardly produce a retardation of three units. In the first case, in fact, the human intervention operates in the same direction as time, which expects as much, so to speak. Mediner argued that Field C was such that it could operate in both directions; and an error in maintenance or a breakdown of some minor mechanism was sufficient to reverse the effect of the emission. In this case, instead of extending life to twice its average length, the machine would devour it precipitously. In the space of a few minutes, the citizens of Diacosia would age decades. And there followed the mathematical proof.

After Edwin Mediner's revelation, a wave of panic swept through the city of longevity. A few people, overlooking the risk of abruptly reentering an "accelerated environment," took flight. But Cristofari's assurances about the efficiency of the installation and the very fact that nothing had happened placated the anxieties. Life in Diacosia continued its monotonous succession of identical, placid, colorless days. Pleasures were weak and insipid, the throbbing delirium of love lacked the overpowering force it once had, news, voices, even the music that came from the outside world were now unpleasant because of their great speed. In a word, life was less interesting, despite the constant distractions. And yet this boredom was slight when compared to the thought that tomorrow, when one by one their contemporaries would pass away, the citizens of Diacosia would still be young and strong; and then their contemporaries' children would gradually die off, but the Diacosians would be full of vigor; and even their contemporaries' grandchildren and great-grandchildren would leave the world, and they who were still alive, with decades of good years ahead of them, would read the obituary notices. This was the thought that dominated the community, that calmed restless spirits, that resolved jealousies and quarrels; this was why they were not agonized as before by the passage of time and the future presented itself as a vast landscape and when confronted by disappointment men and women told themselves: Why worry about it? I'll think about it tomorrow, there isn't any hurry.

After two years, the population had climbed to 52,000, and already the first generation of Diacosians had been born. They would reach full maturity at forty. After ten years, more than 120,000 creatures swarmed over that square kilometer, and slowly, much more slowly than in other cities where time galloped, the skyline rose to dizzying heights. Diacosia had now become the greatest wonder of the world. Caravans of tourists lined the periphery, observing through the gates those people who were so different, who moved with the slowness of MS victims succumbing to paralysis.

The phenomenon lasted twenty years. And a few seconds were enough to destroy it. How did the tragedy occur? Was it caused by a man's will? Or was it chance? Perhaps one of the technicians, anguished by love or illness, wanted to abbreviate his torment and set the catastrophe in motion. Or was he maddened simply from exasperation with that empty, egocentric life, concerned only with self-preservation? And so he purposely reversed the effect of the machine, freeing the vandal forces of time.

It was May 17th, a warm, sunny day. In the fields, along the fence that ran around the perimeter, hundreds of curious observers were stationed, their eyes riveted to people just like them, whose life passed twice as slowly. From within the city came the thin, harmonious voice of the antenna. It had a bell-like resonance. The present writer was there that day and he observed a group of four children playing with a ball. "How old are you?" I asked the oldest one. "Last month I was twenty," she answered politely, but with exaggerated slowness. And their way of running was strange: all soft, viscous movements, like a film shot in slow motion. Even the ball had less bounce for them.

Beyond the fence were the lawns and paths of a garden; the barrier surrounding the buildings began at about fifty meters. A breeze moved the leaves in the trees, yet languidly, it seemed, as if they were leaden. Suddenly, about three in the afternoon, the remote hum of the antenna grew more intense and rose like a siren, an unbearable piercing whistle. I will never forget what happened. Even today, at a distance of years, I awake in the dead of night with a start, confronting that horrible vision.

Before my eyes the four children stretched monstrously. I saw them grow, fatten, become adults. Beards sprouted from male chins. Transformed this way and half naked, their childhood clothes having split under the pressure of the lightning growth, they were seized with terror. They opened their mouths to speak, but what came out was a strange noise I had never heard before. In the vortex of unleashed time, the syllables all ran together, like a record played at a higher, mad speed. That gurgling quickly turned into a wheeze, then a desperate shout.

The four children looked around for help, saw us and rushed toward the railing. But life burned inside them; at the railing, a matter of seven or eight seconds, four old people arrived, with white hair and beards, flaccid and bony. One managed to seize the fence with his skeletal hands. He collapsed at once, together with his companions. They were dead. And the decrepit bodies of those poor children immediately gave off a foul odor. They were decomposing, flesh fell away, bones appeared, even the bones—before my very eyes—dissolved into a whitish dust.

Only then did the fatal scream of the machine subside and finally fall silent. Mediner's prophecy came true. For reasons that will forever remain unknown, the time machine had reversed its operation, and a few seconds were enough to swallow three or four centuries of life.

Now a gloomy, sepulchral silence has frozen the city. The

shadow of abject old age has fallen over the skyscrapers, which had just been resplendent with glory and hope. The walls are wrinkled; ominous lines and creases have appeared, oozing black liquids amid a fringe of rotting spider webs. And there is dust everywhere. Dust, stillness, silence. Of the two hundred thousand wealthy, fortunate people who had wanted to live for centuries there remains nothing but white dust, collecting here and there, as on millennial tombs.

(1954)

The
Five
Brothers

On his return from a long journey, Prince Caramasàn was crossing the desert with his retinue and from one hour to the next was expecting the towers of his city to whiten the horizon when he came across an old, naked hermit sitting on a rock. The hermit was so emaciated that the most minute details of his skeleton were visible beneath his skin. Various pilgrims had gathered around him, some kneeling, others standing, most of them hooded, since they had come to free themselves of weighty secrets and were ashamed to show their faces.

Caramasàn, who was a pious prince, did not fail to offer his services to the old man. "Holy hermit," he said, "perhaps God has guided my steps to this place so that you can refresh yourself. After so much penance, do you not need water to drink, or food, or anything else?"

"I thank you, Prince Caramasàn," answered the hermit, "but the benevolence of the Eternal One has thus far spared me the pains of hunger and thirst. All the same, to show my gratitude, I shall tell you something: Do you see that cloud growing fainter down there, in the direction of the city?"

Caramasàn looked but saw nothing.

"Your eyes," said the hermit, "are not sharp enough. But this is no time to waste in discussions. The one who is raising the dust is Ubu Murru, the sorcerer, the evil genie, and he is galloping toward your palace. I saw him pass by a little while ago, and I asked him: 'Where are you going in such haste, cursed demon?' And he said: 'I am going to the house of Caramasàn to take away his five sons. In fact, it is written that if Ubu Murru succeeds in surprising the five brothers Caramasàn together, he will be able to drive them to Hell with him. If, however, one of the five is absent, Ubu Murru will not have any power over them. I know that today they have gathered to attend their father's return. And so I will be able to steal them away.'

"This was Ubu Murru's answer," proceeded the hermit, "and the evil one cannot lie to me. Therefore, honest prince, mount the best horse in your stable and hurry, if you want to see your sons alive again. Ubu Murru is riding at breakneck speed, but you must ride even faster. Follow him, overtake him, precede him across the threshold of your palace."

Stricken with anguish, Caramasàn thanked the hermit for the warning and leaped on the back of his most trusty charger, a black Persian horse so fast that he was christened Lover's Desire. He left the caravan and hurried away much to the pilgrims' amazement.

Under the spur the horse splendidly devoured great stretches of the desert, but there was no trace of Ubu Murru. And Caramasàn had already fallen into despair when on the far horizon he spied a tiny plume of dust. "On, on, Lover's Desire!" pleaded the prince, and the horse again increased his speed, although he felt his heart bursting. The plume became a little cloud, the cloud a thick billow of sand, and finally Caramasàn had a close look at Ubu Murru. His skin was blackish, and he rode bareback like an Indian, his great mane of shaggy hair waving behind him like a flag.

In the heat of the race, the eight hooves, now equal, beat the crust of the desert so hard that the noise could be heard from a distance. The prince knew that his horse had now given everything he had and could not hold up much longer. So he thought he would resort to cunning, and bowing over one of the animal's ears, he whispered: "For the love of God, make one last effort and carry us ahead of that rider." The horse in fact made one last effort and bolted ahead of Ubu Murru, who was left biting the dust. Then Prince Caramasàn quickly slipped off his broad silver belt and threw it behind him. Ubu Murru's horse tangled his hooves in it and collapsed on the desert stones with a thump that sounded like thunder.

In this way the prince outstripped the ill-omened spirit and no longer needed to mistreat his horse to reach his palace first. There he found his five sons waiting for him. They were named alphabetically, in descending order of age: Andrea, Barnabo, Calisto, Dario, and Enrico. After the customary greetings, he told them: "Unfortunately, my sons, the pleasure of your company has not been granted to me. In the desert, a half day's journey from here, I encountered a hermit who made me a revelation." And he explained everything to them.

When Caramasàn finished his story—throughout which he stood near a window and repeatedly glanced to the street to see if Ubu Murru was about to arrive—the five sons were quickly separated for fear that the evil genie might surprise them together. "I shall go to the mountains," announced Andrea, the first-born. "I shall retire to the seacoast," said Barnabo, the second son. And so on, with the other three also choosing different residences to insure that they would never all meet in the same place. A few minutes later Prince Caramasàn, who on his journey had so often sighed for his sons' company, found himself alone once again. And he was not much comforted by the sight of Ubu Murru, who, beaten and worn-out, walked through the streets, leading his even more battered horse.

From that day on Caramasàn's five sons lived apart for fear of death, although their love for one another was just as strong as ever. Only rarely did they meet, after taking many precautions, and never more than four of them at a time. It was a source of great suffering to their father.

But the years passed with their frightening quickness and the time came for Prince Caramasàn to die. Feeling himself very close to the end, he ordered a messenger: "Summon my five sons. And tell them to rush to their old father, who is about to leave this earth."

The five brothers consulted one another by letter. How could they avoid Ubu Murru surprising them all united at their father's deathbed? Thus it was decided that for their common safety, one of the five, chosen by lot, would remain far from the city. And the lot fell to Calisto, the third-born son.

Unfortunately, old age and sickness had so clouded Prince Caramasàn's memory that he no longer remembered the hermit's warning. Seeing only four sons around his bed, he said: "I see Andrea, Barnabo, Dario, and Enrico, but I do not see Calisto. Where is Calisto? Is he perhaps not interested in the death of his old father?"

Andrea was about to provide an explanation when the others poked him in the ribs. So he fell silent. Caramasàn, believing that they were unable to justify their brother's absence, lifted an emaciated hand and said: "Calisto has not fulfilled a son's most sacred duty. Therefore I disinherit him. My wealth will be divided among you four alone." And after several general recommendations, he took his last breath.

When Calisto learned of what happened, he sent to ask his brothers: "Why did you not explain to our father the reason for my absence? I would have been spared his unjust reproaches. However, let me know when I can come to take my share of the inheritance." The brothers answered: "What inheritance can you claim? Our father disowned you, in the presence of many witnesses." And they did not give him a penny.

Poor Calisto's grief and rage were such as to drive him to the brink of madness. Reduced to poverty, he gave himself over to brigandage, planning, at the cost of his own life, to surprise his brothers gathered together and thus bring their number to five; then would Ubu Murru come to seize them.

So the others began to fear him. And their meetings became even more infrequent. New precautions were taken: they now decided that no more than three of them should meet at any one time, since if the four brothers were together Calisto might come upon them, forming the fatal number.

But this was not enough. Little by little the brothers grew to abhor one another's presence, which, they somehow reasoned, was the origin of the danger. If it were necessary to move from one place to another, each of them sent his servants ahead to investigate whether one of his brothers were there, in which case they would forego the journey.

Thus a mutual hatred was born. And in this life of anxiety only one hope remained, namely, that at least one of the brothers might die. Hence to the fear of an encounter was added, even more insane, the fear of being murdered; and the brothers plotted against one another, devising ambushes, traps, and poisonous draughts.

Until one day Andrea, no longer willing to tolerate such a precarious and humiliating situation, returned to the desert to seek the hermit's counsel. In the desert he found the rock and on the rock sat a penitent. Yet it was not the old hermit his father had described, but a young man who smiled pleasantly. And around him stood various other pilgrims, all of whom were hooded because they had come there to free themselves of weighty secrets and were ashamed to show their faces.

Andrea approached the young man's feet, and bowing down, he asked: "Holy hermit, do you know where I can find the old anchorite who once sat where you are now sitting?" Then he related the entire story.

"Unhappy prince," answered the young man without hesitation, "your father and his five sons have been the victims of a deception. The old man with whom your father spoke was not a hermit. It was Ubu Murru himself, the sorcerer, the evil genie, disguised as an ascetic. And when your father rushed away to reach his palace as quickly as possible, the demon flew ahead of him, assuming the form of a galloping rider. He did not have any power over you. His lie was intended only to sow discord and hatred among you. And today he triumphs. Go on, Prince Andrea, hurry to your brothers, embrace them, and reveal the deception to them."

At these words Andrea lifted a prayer of gratitude to heaven, since his afflictions had come to an end. In that same moment four of the other pilgrims who had heard the revelation removed their hoods and with equal exultation intoned a hymn to the Eternal One. Then one of them approached Andrea and said, sobbing, "Embrace me. Do you not recognize your brother Barnabo?" And the remaining three did likewise.

But looking at one another, the five brothers felt every joy vanish. In the course of those years they had grown old, and behind them stood a long, wretched life of fear and hatred, nor was there any time to make amends. The sun was about to descend behind the horizon of the desert, and from the opposite side the shadows of night were advancing.

(1954)

The Flying Carpet

One fine day, after the noble Bessarione family had been overwhelmed by debts, their creditors descended like vultures to divide what remained of the estate. And in the very castle where the family had led a princely life for centuries, an auction was held.

The ravenous antique dealers arrived from the city in limousines. Wearing furs and camel overcoats because of the cold, they sat like schoolchildren on the rows of benches set up in the immense vestibule. There were also some people who were simply curious, merchants and brokers from the area.

The objects up for auction included furniture, paintings, tapestries, clocks, armor, silver, swords, lamps, vases, miniatures, engravings, spinning wheels, chess sets, hourglasses, umbrella stands, riding gear, books, and porcelain. Gradually, it was all swallowed up by the buyers. The selling went very quickly and the auctioneer, Professor Claudio Ger, did not need to tire himself with long sales pitches: so intense was the bidding.

Until it came the turn of a small, red and blue rectangular carpet with a very detailed design. The auctioneer signalled to the attendants with a nod, as he had done with each of the most important pieces, and they carried the carpet around the room so that everyone could admire it. Then he began his description.

"This carpet," he said, "as you will no doubt have realized at first glance, is an extraordinary specimen. . . . Only six or seven such articles are known to exist. . . . It displays the famous workmanship of Esckhen, who flourished for a brief time during the eleventh century and vanished without leaving a trace. . . . For you, who are much more astute in these things than I, further comment would be pointless. . . . It is my duty to inform you that the base price for this carpet is the *sine qua non* for the sale. . . . Ladies and gentlemen, the bidding will begin at one million lire."

An emphatic murmuring, obviously ironic, echoed through the room.

"Hem, hem," added Ger, clearing his voice, "a legend is attached to this carpet. . . . Among the Bessariones, it is told how the progenitor of the family brought it home as plunder after a crusade or some similar expedition . . . and it is said that this is no less than a magical carpet that flies, precisely one of those mentioned in *The Arabian Nights*, with which all of you are of course familiar."

Suppressed snickers were heard here and there around the room.

The auctioneer raised an envelope until everyone could see it: "And here, printed on a slip of paper, are the four formulas needed to raise the carpet, make it turn right and left, and descend."

The snickers turned to unrestrained laughter.

"You, old Giacomo," the auctioneer continued, unperturbed, turning to a decrepit peasant who was standing on one side of the room, "you were a witness. Tell these skeptical ladies and gentlemen a little about it."

Then old Giacomo came forward and in a very uncertain Italian related that more than once, and with his own eyes, he had seen Count Arduino Bessarione take off on the carpet; that usually the said count stood up straight on the carpet, although sometimes he sat down on it too; that the count used it only at night, for brief incursions into Paris, since he was quite fond of the ladies and the gay life; that in the morning, when Giacomo entered the count's room to clean it, he always found him asleep in his bed, and the carpet lay in its usual place; that one morning, however, he did not find him in bed, although the carpet was there, and no more was ever heard of the count; that the only explanation for the incident was that the count might have been a little tipsy on his return trip from Paris that night and he fell asleep on the carpet, whereupon a strong wind made him slip off and the riderless carpet returned home by itself.

There was more laughter, and salacious comments punctuated the story. All the same, several people were visibly impressed.

"Could we not," suggested the harsh voice of Commendatore Jackia, the dean of the antiquaries who were present, "could we not have a demonstration before the bidding?"

"Most assuredly," answered the auctioneer. "To facilitate the take-off, ladies and gentlemen, we should go out onto the terrace."

They went outside, and the carpet was spread on the ground. "Who would like to try it?" asked Ger, unfolding the slip of paper. "Here are the formulas. . . . They are difficult to read, but very brief."

Everyone was now strolling around the small carpet and looking at it with curiosity, careful not to touch it with their feet. Then they stared at one another, winking and smiling idiotically.

"Who would like to try it?" repeated Ger, looking around for an appropriate subject. "Don't you feel tempted, Melloni?"

Melloni was a noted collector of ceramics. "Me?" he said, embarrassed. "How many passengers can fit on this carpet?"

"It is a one-seater, a typical one-seater . . ."

"Then I must go alone?" Melloni was obviously trying to extricate himself. "But . . . who knows how cold it is up there . . . and then there isn't even a seat belt. . . . I must confess that—"

At this point the young Baron Menincalzo came forward: he was the owner of an estate in the area, an athletic fellow who had run in the annual marathon the year before. "I shall go!" he announced solemnly and walked onto the carpet.

But his wife, who was very jealous, seized him by an arm. "You? What do you think you're doing? Don't go playing the martyr now, please be quiet!" And she pulled him off the carpet without his making the slightest show of resistance (a little later they were seen leaving the castle).

"Well," the corpulent Commendatore Jackia intervened again, "seeing that the young people are so cautious, I would try it if you think—"

"I would be honored," said Ger. "Please, right this way, Commendatore. . . . Yes, that's it. . . . Very well. Here, it's better to sit down. . . . And now for the formulas."

Jackia was sitting on the carpet in the lotus position: he took the slip of paper, put on his glasses, read it once, twice, made himself more comfortable, looked around, smiled, reddened, and finally began to utter the magic words:

A mor dor sè
tita sela te lé . . .

But at this point he leaped to his feet and like a restive horse bolted a couple of meters from the carpet. He was breathless: "Oh, oh . . . I felt a shudder . . . just a shudder . . ." And then he berated the auctioneer: "You try, my dear sir, you fly it, you who seem so sure of yourself."

"Me? Me?" said Ger, as if he had suffered some terrible offense. Night fell and they were still there discussing the matter, but no one dared to take a ride.

After a few days I carried away the carpet for a pittance. And I still have it in my house, in the living room. Every morning the maid cleans it on the balcony with a carpet beater.

And me? you will no doubt ask. Have I tried to fly it? No, I haven't tried it. Why? I refuse to answer. Fear, you say? You may think that I am afraid if you like, but so what?

As far as the carpet is concerned, it is quiet and good and can usually be found lying on the parquet floor. It doesn't move, doesn't complain. Yet every so often, at two or three in the morning, from the bedroom I hear it fidget a little, like a dog who cannot find the right position to sleep in.

I get up, go to the living room and turn on the light. The carpet lies motionless, but one corner is folded up, into a kind of scroll. Three hours ago, when I went to bed, this fold wasn't there.

(1955)

The Prohibited Word

From veiled hints, allusive jokes, discreet circumlocutions, vague whispers, I have finally gotten the idea that in this city, where I moved three months ago, there exists a prohibition against using a word. Which one? I don't know. It could be a strange, unusual word, but it could also be rather common, in which case it would cause some inconvenience for someone in my line of work.

Curious more than alarmed, I went to talk to my friend Hieronimo, who is among the wisest people I know. Since he has lived in this city for more than twenty years, he is quite familiar with everything about it.

"It is true," he told me at once. "We are prohibited from using a word, and everyone avoids it."

"And which word is it?"

"You see," he said to me, "I know you are an honest person, I know I can trust you. And I am sincerely your friend. Yet despite all this, believe me, it would be better if I didn't tell you. Listen: I have lived in this city for over twenty years, it has welcomed me, given me work, it lets me lead a decent life—we shouldn't forget these things. And me? For my part, I have faithfully obeyed the laws, good or bad as they might be. Who has stopped me from leaving? Nevertheless, I have stayed. I don't want to play the philosopher, and I certainly don't want to mimic Socrates when it was suggested that he escape from prison, but I really am averse to breaking the rules of the city that considers me its son. . . . It may seem like such a minute point. God knows, then, if it is really so minute—"

"But we can talk here with complete   No one can hear us. Come on now, Hieronimo, won't you tell me this blessed word? Who could denounce you? Me?"

"I notice," observed Hieronimo with an ironic smile, "that you see things with the mentality of our forefathers. You seem to be referring to the threat of punishment. And indeed, once it was believed that without punishment the law could not have any coercive effectiveness. This may have even been true. But it is a crude and rather primitive idea. Even though the law may not be accompanied by a penalty, it can still achieve its maximum value; we have evolved."

"What restrains you, then? Conscience? The prospect of remorse?"

"Oh, conscience! You poor old ironmonger. For many years you have certainly rendered men invaluable services, but even you have had to change with the times. You have now been transformed into something that resembles you only vaguely, something simpler, more standard, more tranquil, I would say, but far less compelling and tragic."

"If you don't give me a better explanation—"

"We lack a scientific definition. It is popularly called 'conformity.' It is the peace enjoyed by the person who feels in harmony with the masses that besiege him. Or else it is the anxiety, the uneasiness, the confusion of anyone who deviates from the norm."

"But is this enough?"

"Of course it is! Conformity is a tremendous force, more powerful than nuclear weapons. Naturally, it isn't the same everywhere.

There exists a geography of conformity. In the underdeveloped countries it is still in its infancy, in embryo, or is unfolding in a disorderly way, capriciously, without direction. Fashion is a typical example. In the most advanced countries, however, this force has now penetrated every sphere of experience, it is completely consolidated, it is suspended, one might say, in the very atmosphere: and it is in the hands of power."

"And how are we doing?"

"Not too bad, in fact not bad at all. The prohibition against the word, for example, was a sagacious initiative designed by the authorities precisely to determine how far the people's conformity has matured. Thus it was a sort of test. And the results showed that we have reached a high level of maturity, much higher than anticipated. That word is now taboo. No matter how hard you search for it, I guarantee that you will absolutely not find it here among us, not even in the criminal underworld. People adapted to the prohibition in no time at all. And there was no need to threaten them with denunciations, fines, or imprisonment."

"If all you say is true, then it would be very easy to make everyone become honest."

"Certainly. But it will take many years, decades, perhaps centuries. It is obviously easy to prohibit a word, since giving up one word doesn't cost much effort. But fraud, malicious gossip, vice, crime, anonymous letters are more serious. . . . People have grown fond of them, just try to suggest that they give them up. These are indeed sacrifices. Besides, if from the start a spontaneous wave of conformity is left to itself, it will lead to evil, brutish complacency, compromise, villainy. It is necessary to change people's orientation, and it isn't easy. We will succeed in time, of course, you can be certain we will."

"And do you find this desirable? Does it not produce a levelling, a frightening uniformity?"

"Desirable? It can't be called desirable. It is rather useful, extremely useful. The collectivity benefits from it. Who ever suspected that the characters, the 'types,' the striking personalities that until yesterday had been so idolized and fascinating were after all nothing more than the first germs of unlawfulness and anarchy? Do they not represent a flaw in the social fabric? And, on the other hand, have you

ever noticed that among the most aggressive people there is an extraordinary, almost distressing uniformity of character traits?"

"In short, you have decided not to tell me this word?"

"My son, you mustn't take it like that. You should realize that it
is not because of mistrust. If I told it to you, I would feel uneasy."

"You too? Even a highly gifted man like you has been reduced to
the level of the masses?"

"So it goes, my friend," and he shook his head dejectedly. "We
would have to be titans to resist the pressure of the environment."

"And what about   ? The supreme good! Once you loved it.
You would have done anything to avoid losing it. And now?"

"Anything, anything whatever . . . Plutarch's heroes . . . it
would take better men than they. . . . Even the most noble sentiment
atrophies and gradually dissolves if no one pays any more attention to
it. The sad fact is that we cannot desire paradise by ourselves."

"So: don't you want to tell me? Is it a dirty word? Or does it have
some criminal significance?"

"On the contrary. It is a clean word, honest and very calm. And
these very qualities demonstrate the legislators' subtlety. There already was a tacit, if rather mild, prohibition against obscene or inde-
cent words. . . . There was discretion, a good education. The experiment would not have had much value."

"At least tell me if it's a noun, adjective, verb, adverb."

"But why do you insist so? If you stay here with us, one fine day
you too will identify the prohibited word, all of a sudden, almost
without noticing it. So it goes, my son. You will absorb it from the
air."

"Well, old Hieronimo, you are really a stubborn fellow. Never
mind. It means that to satisfy my curiosity I will have to go to the library and consult the Unique Texts. There must be a record of the
law, right? They must have printed it! And it will clearly state the prohibited word!"

"You still haven't taken that step forward, you are still following
the old line of reasoning. You are also ingenuous. A law that prohibits
the use of a word by using it would automatically contravene itself. It
would be a juridical monstrosity. It is useless for you to go to a library."

"Come on, Hieronimo, you're making fun of me! Someone still must have decreed that from such and such a day on word X is prohibited. And he would have had to use it, right? Otherwise how would the people have been informed?"

"This is indeed the aspect of the case that is perhaps slightly problematic. There are three theories: there are those who say that undercover police spread the prohibition by word of mouth; others assert that at their homes they found sealed envelopes that contained the decree of the prohibition with the order to burn it as soon as it was read. And then there are the integralists—you would call them pessimists—who simply maintain that there was no need for an explicit order, since the citizens are easily led in such matters; it was enough for the authorities to wish the law into effect and everyone knew it at once, through a sort of telepathy."

"But everyone didn't become a worm. However small their numbers, there must still exist, here in this city, some independent people who think their own thoughts. There must be some opponents, heretics, rebels, outlaws—call them what you will. Does it not seem likely that some of them will utter or write the prohibited word as an act of defiance? What happens then?"

"Nothing, absolutely nothing. This is precisely the reason for the extraordinary success of the experiment. The prohibition has entered the people's souls so deeply that it has influenced their sense perception."

"What do you mean?"

"That through a veto of the unconscious, which is always ready to intervene in dangerous situations, if someone utters the nefarious word, people *do not hear it* anymore, and if they find it written, they *do not see it*."

"And what do they see in place of the word?"

"Nothing, a bare wall, if it is written on a wall; a blank space, if it is written on paper."

I tried one last assault: "Hieronimo, please, just out of curiosity: while I was talking with you today, here, did I at any time use this mysterious word? You can at least tell me this; you won't lose anything by it."

Old Hieronimo smiled and winked.

"Then I did use it?"

He winked again.

But a sovereign sadness suddenly darkened his face.

"How many times? Don't play hard to get now, come on, tell me, how many times?"

"I don't know how many, really, my word of honor. Even if you had used it, I couldn't have heard it. But it seemed to me that at a certain point—although I swear I don't remember when—there was a pause, a very brief moment of silence, as if you had uttered a word and the sound didn't reach me. It might also have been an involuntary interruption, as always happens in conversations."

"Only once?"

"Oh enough already! Don't insist."

"Do you know what I'm going to do, then? As soon as I get back home, I plan to transcribe this conversation, word for word, and then send it to the printer."

"To what end?"

"If what you have said is true, the printer, who we can assume is a good citizen, will not see the prohibited word. Thus there are two possibilities: either he will leave an empty space in the line where the word appears and this will explain everything, or the line will be set straight without any empty space, in which case I need only compare the printed version with the original (which I will keep, naturally) to learn which word has been omitted."

Hieronimo laughed amiably.

"You'll be wasting your time, my friend. No matter what printer you employ, conformity is such that he will automatically know how to act so as to evade your little trick. That is to say, he *will see*, just once, the word you have written—assuming that you in fact write it—and he will not skip it when he sets the type. You can be sure that the printers here are well trained and very informed."

"Forgive me, but what is the point of all this? Would it not benefit the city if I learned the prohibited word without anyone saying or writing it?"

"For the time being, probably not. From the conversation you have had with me, it is clear that you are not mature. An initiation is required. In a word, you have still not conformed. You are still not worthy—according to the reigning orthodoxy—to respect the law."

"And what about my readers? Won't they recognize anything if they read this dialogue?"

"They will simply see an empty space. And they will simply think: how careless, they left out a word."

(1958)

The
Plague

One September morning—by chance I was present—a gray car drove into the Iris Garage on Via Mendoza. The car was an exotic make with a rather unusual body, and it had foreign plates with which I was entirely unfamiliar.

The owner of the garage, myself, the old head mechanic Celada, who is my best friend, and the other workers were all in the office. The huge parking lot on the ground floor was visible through a window.

A gentleman about forty years old got out of the car. He was tall, blond, very elegant, slightly stoop-shouldered. He looked around, troubled. The engine had not been turned off and it was idling. Nevertheless, it made a strange noise that I had never heard before, a dry screeching, as if the cylinders were grinding stones.

At once I saw how Celada's face went pale. "Holy Madonna," he murmured. "This is the plague. Like in Mexico. I remember it well." Then he ran up to the strange man, who was a foreigner and did not understand a word of Italian. Still, the mechanic was able to explain himself with a few gestures, so anxious was he for the man to leave. And the foreigner left, his car constantly emitting that horrendous noise.

"You've got a lot of nerve," the owner said to the mechanic when he returned to the office. Having heard them hundreds of times, we recognized only too well Celada's implausible stories about his trip to the Americas in his youth.

The mechanic was not offended. "You'll see," he said. "This is going to be serious for us."

The episode, as I later learned, was the first sign of disaster, the timid tolling that was only a prelude to the full death knell.

But three weeks passed before another symptom appeared. This was an ambiguous statement from the municipal government: it announced that to prevent "abuses and irregularities," special squads had been instituted within the highway patrol and the traffic police to inspect the efficiency of public and private auto vehicles both at the owners' domiciles and at garages and, where necessary, to order their "preventive sequestration" immediately. It was impossible to guess the real motive behind such vague terms, and people paid no attention to the announcement. Who could have guessed that those "inspectors" might be nothing but officials appointed to remove corpses in times of plague?

It took two more days for the fear to catch fire. Then the news, however implausible it might have seemed, spread from one end of the city to the other with lightning speed: the auto plague had arrived.

There was endless talk about the various warning signs and manifestations of the mysterious illness. It was said that the infection first revealed itself with a hollow resonance in the engine, like congestion from a cold. Then the joints swelled into monstrous bulges, every surface was covered with yellow, foul-smelling incrustations, and finally the entire engine was turned into a confused tangle of crushed rods, shafts, and gears.

It was claimed that the contagion spread through exhaust fumes, so drivers avoided heavily travelled roads, the center of the city was practically deserted, and silence, which had been invoked for so long, established its ghostly reign there. Oh, where were the festive klaxon and thundering exhaust of better days?

Most public garages were also abandoned because of the promiscuity they involved. Anyone who did not possess his own garage preferred to leave his car in less infected areas, like the fields on the outskirts of the city. Beyond the race track, the sky was reddened from the fires for cars that had been killed by the plague and piled up to burn in a vast enclosure, which people called the lazar house.

As was inevitable, the worst excesses were unleashed: unguarded cars were stolen and stripped; there were anonymous denunciations of cars that were actually healthy, but that were nonetheless towed away and consigned to the flames because suspicion had been aroused; inspectors charged with the examination and sequestration of vehicles abused their offices; there was the criminal recklessness of those who knew that their cars were infected, but still drove around in them, spreading the contagion; and suspected autos were burned alive (the terrible screams could be heard from afar).

In the beginning, the panic was in fact worse than the danger. It is calculated that in the first month not more than 5,000 of the 20,000 automobiles in our province succumbed to the pestilence. Then there seemed to be a respite, which was bad, because it created the illusion that the plague had all but ended and a mass of cars returned to circulation, thus multiplying the chances for infection.

Then the disease reasserted itself with exacerbated fury. The spectacle of cars struck by the plague became commonplace on the road. The soft rumble of the engine suddenly rippled and cracked, shattering into a frenetic metallic crash. There were a few tremors, then the car stopped, reduced to a smoking wreck. The agony endured by trucks was even more horrible, since their powerful viscera put up a desperate fight. Lugubrious splashes and roars issued from those monsters, until a kind of sibilant howl announced the dishonorable end.

At that time I was a chauffeur employed by a rich widow, Marchesa Rosanna Finamore, who lived with a nephew in the family's old villa. I was doing very well there. One could not say that the pay was princely, but I could find consolation in the fact that the position was practically a sinecure: I did little driving during the day, even less at night, and I was entrusted with the maintenance of the car. This was a huge black Rolls-Royce, and although it was indeed a veteran of many expeditions, its appearance was incomparably aristocratic. I was proud of it. On the road, even the fastest sports cars repressed their habitual arrogance when that ancient sarcophagus came into view oozing blue blood. And the engine, notwithstanding its age, was no less than a miracle. In a word, I loved the car more than if it were my own.

Hence I too was troubled by the epidemic. Of course it was said that high-performance vehicles were virtually immune. But how could one be certain? On my advice, moreover, the marchesa stopped going out during the day, when it was easy to catch the disease, and limited the use of the car to rare outings after dinner, such as concerts, lectures, or visits.

One night, near the end of September, precisely at the height of the plague, we were returning home in the Rolls-Royce after chatting with the usual ladies to lighten the melancholy of that time. Just as we entered Piazza Bismarck, I perceived, in the harmonious rustle of the engine, a brief knock followed by a harsh scratching that lasted for a fraction of a second. I asked the marchesa about it.

"I didn't hear anything," she told me. "Just watch the turns, Giovanni, and don't worry about it. This old jalopy isn't afraid of anything."

Nevertheless, before we arrived home, that sinister knock, or obstruction, or friction—I did not know exactly what to call it—occurred two more times, filling me with anxiety. After we returned, I stayed in the small garage a long time, contemplating the noble machine, which was apparently asleep. But then certain indescribable moans began to come from the hood at regular intervals, even though the engine had been turned off, and I was certain of the worst.

What to do? I thought of asking the advice of the old mechanic Celada who, apart from the Mexican experience, claimed to know of a special mixture of mineral oils that had prodigious healing powers. Although it was past midnight, I telephoned the café where he played cards almost every evening. He was there.

"Celada," I told him, "you have always been my friend."

"Well, I hope so."

"We have always gotten along well."

"Thank God."

"Can I trust you?"

"What the devil is going on?"

"Come over, I would like you to have a look at the Rolls-Royce."

"I'll come at once," he said, and I thought I heard a soft laugh before I hung up the phone.

I was sitting on a bench, waiting, as a wheeze issued more and more frequently from the depths of the engine. In my mind I counted Celada's steps, calculating the time; he would be here in a little while. As I was straining my ears to hear if the mechanic had arrived, the shuffle of feet echoed in the courtyard. Yet it was the sound of more than one man. A dreadful suspicion crossed my mind.

And here, opening the garage door, introducing themselves and walking toward me were two pairs of dirty maroon overalls, two exiled faces—in a word, two inspectors. I saw only half of Celada's face: he had hidden behind the door and stood there, watching.

"You filthy swine! . . . Get out of here, damn you!" I breathlessly searched for a weapon—a monkey wrench, a metal bar, a walking stick. But they were already upon me, and I was soon held prisoner in those brawny arms.

"You bastards!" I screamed, my face contorted with rage and derision. "Rebel against the city government, against the public functionaries! Rebel against those who work for the good of the city!" They bound me to the bench after having slipped into my pocket—what supreme mockery!—the standard form for "preventive sequestration." Finally they drove away the Rolls-Royce, which withdrew with a painful whimpering, yet full of sovereign dignity. It seemed as if it wanted to say goodbye to me.

When, after half an hour of tremendous effort, I managed to free myself, I dashed into the night without even notifying my employer of the incident and ran like a madman to the lazar house beyond the race track, hoping to get there in time.

But just as I arrived, Celada was leaving the gate with the two inspectors, and he slipped away as if he had not seen me, disappearing into the darkness.

I did not succeed in finding him. Nor was I able to enter the enclosure and have the destruction of the Rolls-Royce delayed. I stood there a long time with an eye glued to a crack in the fence. I saw the pyre of unfortunate cars; dark shapes were writhing in agony amid the flames. Where was mine? It was impossible to distinguish in that inferno. Only for an instant, above the savage howl of the blazing fire, did I think that I recognized its dear voice; it was a shrill, heartrending shout, which soon vanished into nothing.

(1958)

Confidential

Dear Editor,

It depends only on you whether this confession I am painfully forced to make will lead to my salvation or to my utter shame, dishonor, and ruin.

It is a long story, and not even I know how I managed to keep it a secret. My family, friends, and colleagues have never had the slightest suspicion of it.

I must go back to the beginning, almost thirty years ago. At that time I was an ordinary reporter at the newspaper that you now direct. I was conscientious, willing, diligent, but I did not distinguish myself in any way. At night, when I gave the city editor my brief reports on robberies, highway accidents, and ceremonies, I almost always endured the mortification of seeing them butchered: entire sentences were cut and completely rewritten; there were corrections, deletions, insertions, and interpolations of every kind. Despite my suffering, I knew that the city editor did not do these things maliciously. On the contrary. The fact is that I was (and am) not permitted to write. And if they didn't fire me, it was only because of my zeal in gathering news throughout the city.

Nevertheless, a desperate literary ambition burned in the depths of my soul. And when a colleague who was slightly younger than I published an article, or when a contemporary brought out a book, and I noticed that both the article and the book were successful, envy bit into my bowels like a poisoned claw.

Now and then I tried to imitate these privileged ones by writing sketches, lyrical pieces, stories. But every time, the pen fell from my hand after the first few lines. I reread what I had written, and I realized that the thing couldn't stand up. Then I was seized by fits of discouragement and bitterness. Luckily, they didn't last long. My foolish literary aspirations were appeased again; I found distraction in my work, thought of other things, and in the end life went on serenely enough.

Until one day a man I had not seen before came looking for me at the newspaper. He must have been about forty years old; he was short and quite stout, with a sleepy, inexpressive face. He could have easily proved odious if he had not been so good-natured, polite, modest. His extreme humility was the most striking thing about him. He said that his name was Ileano Bissat; he lived in Trento and was the uncle of an old schoolmate of mine. He was married and had two daughters. He had lost his job in a warehouse because of illness and he didn't know which way to turn to make a little money. "So what can I do about it?" I asked.

"I have a weakness for writing," he answered, cowering at the revelation. "I have written a sort of novel and some stories. Enrico [that is to say, my old schoolmate] has read them and said that they aren't bad. He advised me to come and see you. You work for a large newspaper, you know people, you have contacts, authority, you could—"

"Me? But I'm the bottom rung on the ladder. Besides, the newspaper doesn't publish literary pieces if they are not by recognized writers."

"But you—"

"I am not a writer. I'm an ordinary reporter. That would be the last straw." (And my frustrated literary demon transfixed me with a pin beneath the fourth rib.)

Bissat wore an insinuating smile: "But would you like to write?"

"Of course. To be capable of it!"

"Well, Signor Buzzati, don't give up so easily! You are young, you have time enough ahead of you. You'll see, you'll see. But I have disturbed you enough, I must now be off. Look, I am leaving my sins here with you. If by chance you have half an hour, try to have a look at them. If you don't have the time, it doesn't matter."

"But I tell you again, I can't be useful to you. It isn't a question of good will."

"Who knows?" He was already at the door, making low bows as he left. "Sometimes one thing leads to another. Have a look at them. You may not regret it."

He left a bundle of manuscripts on the table. You can well imagine whether I had any desire to read them. I took them home, where they remained, on top of a bureau, buried in piles of other papers and books for at least a couple of months.

I had stopped thinking about them altogether, when one night I couldn't get to sleep and I was tempted to write a story. To tell the truth, I didn't have many ideas for one, but there was always my damned ambition.

Yet there was no more typing paper in the usual drawer. And I recalled that in the middle of some books, on top of the bureau, there had to be an old notebook I had hardly begun. As I looked for it, I made a pile of papers fall, and they scattered across the floor.

It was chance. While I was picking them up, my glance fell on a typewritten page that had slipped out of a folder. I read a line, two lines, and stopped, my curiosity aroused. I went on to the bottom of the page and looked for the next one and read that as well. Then on and on I read. It was Ileano Bissat's novel.

I was seized by a savage jealousy that after thirty years has still not subsided. What a rotten world! Bissat's writing was strange, new, very beautiful. But perhaps it wasn't very beautiful, perhaps not even good; it may have been simply drivel. The horror was that it corresponded to me, resembled me, affirmed my sense of self. Each piece was one that I would like to have written but was incapable of. I found my world, my tastes, my aversions. I was pleased to death. Did I feel any admiration? No. Only rage, and the most intense rage at that: I was angry that there might be someone who had done those very things I had dreamed of doing since childhood, but to no purpose. Of course, it was an extraordinary coincidence. And as soon as he published his work, that bastard would stand in my way. He would be the first to enter that mysterious kingdom where I, because of a superstitious hope, still deluded myself that I could take the lead. Yet what kind of debut would I have made, even assuming that inspiration had finally come to my assistance? The debut of a plagiarist, a fraud.

Ileano Bissat didn't leave his address. And I couldn't find it. He had to turn up on his own. But what would I tell him?

Another full month passed before he appeared again. He was even more obsequious and modest. "Have you read any of it?"

"I have read it," I told him. But I was doubtful whether to tell him the truth.

"What did you think?"

"Well . . . it isn't bad. But you can't expect this newspaper to—"

"Because I am a nobody?"

"Exactly."

He remained quiet for a few moments, thinking. Then: "But tell me, Signor Buzzati, sincerely. If you were the one who had written these things, instead of me, the nobody, does it seem possible that the newspaper might publish them? You are a member of the staff, you have an in-house position."

"My God, I don't know. The editor is certainly a broad-minded man, and rather adventurous."

His cadaverous face shone with joy: "Well then, why don't we try it?"

"Try what?"

"Listen, sir. Believe me, all I want is a little money. I have no ambitions. If I write, it is only to pass the time. In a word, if you are disposed to help me, I will hand over the whole lot to you."

"What do you mean?"

"I hand everything over to you. It's all yours. Do whatever you want with it. I have written those things, but you can put your name to them. You're young, I'm twenty years older than you, I'm an old man. There is no satisfaction in launching an old man, but the critics gladly bet on the young people who are just starting out. You'll see, we shall enjoy a magnificent success."

"But it would be a scam, a dishonorable exploitation."

"Why? You will pay me. I will use you as a means to place my merchandise. What does it matter to me if the trademark is changed? The account is correct. The important thing is that my writing convinces you."

"It's absurd, absurd. Don't you realize the risk I would be taking? What if it were discovered? And besides, once these pieces are published, once this stock is depleted, what am I going to do?"

"I will stay close to you, naturally. I shall gradually furnish you with another supply. Look in my face. Do you really think I am capable of betraying you? Is this what frightens you? Oh, dear me."

"What if you happen to get sick?"

"For that period you too will be sick."

"What if the newspaper sends me abroad?"

"I shall follow you."

"At my expense?"

"Well, it is only logical. But I am content with very little. I don't have any bad habits."

We debated the thing at length. It was a dishonorable contract, one that would put me at the mercy of a stranger, that involved me in the basest form of extortion, that could drag me into scandal. But the temptation was great, Bissat's writing seemed so beautiful to me, and the mirage of fame exerted such a strong fascination.

The terms of the agreement were simple. Ileano Bissat undertook to write for me whatever I wanted, giving me permission to sign it; to follow and assist me on job-related trips; to keep the entire affair in the strictest confidence; and to avoid writing anything for himself or for a third party. In return, I paid him eighty percent of the earnings. And so the partnership began.

I went to see the editor, your predecessor, and begged him to read one of my stories. He looked at me in a certain way, winked, slipped the piece into a drawer. I withdrew in good order. It was the sort of welcome I had anticipated. I would have been an idiot to expect anything else. But the story (by Ileano Bissat) was first-rate. I had great faith in it.

Four days later the story appeared in the literary section of the newspaper, much to my own and my colleagues' amazement. It was a striking success. But the horrible thing was this: instead of being tormented with shame and remorse, I enjoyed it. And I savored the praise as if it were really for me. I came very close to persuading myself that I had in fact written the story.

Other pieces followed, then the novel, which received a lot of attention. I became a "thing." My first photographs and interviews appeared. I discovered in myself a capacity for lies and impertinence that I had never suspected.

For his part Bissat was irreproachable. When I exhausted the original supply of stories, he furnished me with more, each of which seemed to me more beautiful than the others. And he scrupulously kept himself in the shadows. My misgivings disappeared one by one. I found myself on the crest of a wave. I left the newspaper, became a contributor to the literary section, began to earn huge sums of money. Bissat, who in the meantime had brought into the world three more children, bought himself a villa by the sea and a car.

He was always obsequious and very modest. Not even with veiled allusions did he ever confront me about the glory I enjoyed solely because of him. But he never had enough money. And he sucked my blood.

Contracts are confidential documents, but there are always leaks in the huge publishing houses. Everyone more or less knew that I expected a spectacular heap of banknotes at the end of every month. But they couldn't explain why I wasn't driving a Maserati, why I didn't travel around with young women covered with diamonds and mink, why I didn't own yachts or stables of race horses. What was I doing with all my millions? It was a mystery. And thus was born the legend of my ferocious avarice. An explanation had yet to be found.

This is the situation. And now, dear editor, I come to the point. Ileano Bissat had sworn to me that he had no ambitions, and I believe that this is true. But this is not the source of the threat. The thing is his growing greed for money: for himself, for his children, for their families. He has become a bottomless pit. Eighty percent of the earnings from our publications is no longer enough for him. He has forced me to go into debt up to my neck. And he continues to be unctuous, good-natured, repulsively modest.

Two weeks ago, after thirty years of fraudulent symbiosis, there was a quarrel. He demanded insane additional sums that were not agreed upon. I answered him spitefully. He did not strike back, did not make any threats, did not allude to eventual blackmail. He simply suspended the flow of merchandise. He went on strike. He hasn't written another word. And I am barren of ideas. For more than fifteen days, in fact, the public has been denied the consolation of reading me.

For this reason, sir, I am finally forced to reveal the terrible plot. And to ask forgiveness and clemency. Would you abandon me? Would you want to see cut off forever the career of a man who, whether good or bad, did his best to bring prestige to the newspaper both before and during the fraud? Do you recall some of "my" pieces, which plummeted like fiery meteors into the swampy indifference of the humanity around us? Were they not marvelous? Meet me half-way. A small raise would be enough, I don't know, two or three hundred thousand lire a month. Yes, I think that two hundred thousand would be enough, at least for now. Or else, if worst comes to worst, maybe you could make me a loan? A few million, say? Whatever you do would be for the newspaper. And I would be saved.

Unless you, dear editor, are not the man I have always believed you were. Unless you greet this as a godsend, an opportunity to embarrass me. Do you realize that today you could throw me out without making any settlement at all? You would only have to take this letter and publish it as a story in the literary section without removing a comma.

But no, you won't do it. You have always been a kind-hearted man, incapable of giving the reprobate the slightest push to hurl him into the abyss, even if he deserves it.

And then your newspaper would never publish such a disgusting piece. What can you expect? I myself write like a dog. I get no practice. It isn't my profession. I have nothing at all to do with those stupendous things that Bissat used to furnish me, and that carried my byline.

No, even on the absurd assumption that you might be a wicked man who wants to destroy me, you would never print this disgraceful letter (which cost me so much blood and tears!). The newspaper would sustain too hard a blow from it.

(1966)

Duelling
Stories

The old doctor Nunzio Toro, an exceedingly intelligent and genial man who is nonetheless thought dangerous by some people, loves to entertain his friends with a game he calls "duelling stories." One person begins a story, another intervenes, developing it however he likes, then the first takes another turn, and so on. A player cannot of course prepare his story beforehand: if he did, that would be cheating, and the entire thing would turn into a joke. All the same, Toro is always the one who, one way or another, determines the course of the narrative.

　　Here is an example. He and I are sitting on the porch of his house in the country. It is six in the evening, on a restless day with the sun going in and out of the clouds. As usual he goes first:

An elderly married couple, well-dressed, sad, are talking about their son, who has taken a job in Peru.

"I don't know," says the husband, "the more I think about it, the more I worry. It'll be an unpleasant surprise for him."

"Why unpleasant?"

"Because he doesn't know we're coming, and we'll be a bloody nuisance to him."

"With that immense house he's let!"

"It doesn't matter. You forgot there's his wife, and his wife's family."

"We should've written ahead."

"That's a bright one. Then he could've written right back and told us no."

"Fancy you! Frank is generous. He adores us. You'll see, he'll be happy to see us."

"Enough. Now it's your turn."

I continued:

While these two were talking, a little distance away, a priest was busy writing up the speech he would deliver tomorrow as the inaugural address for an international geophysics conference. It is Monsignor Estogarratz, the noted seismologist, although today, to tell the truth, he is considered past his prime. And he knows it. He also realizes that his appointment as chairman of the conference is due to the support of the "old guard," men like Dorflinger, Stoliepkin, Estancieros, Mandruzzato. And of course his speech cannot disappoint them; if it does, it would be a terrible show of ingratitude. Yet the monsignor believes that his speech shows him to be an adherent of certain avant-garde positions, especially those concerning innovations in the rates of compensation. On the second page, in fact, there is a problematic passage that—

Nunzio Toro's eyes are sparkling.

"Marvelous!" he interrupts me. "The monsignor is an inspired idea. You seem to have read my mind. Now let me continue."

But the seismologist is disturbed by two ladies who are chattering away just behind him. They are about forty years old, still attractive, beautifully tanned.

"Then you saw him too?"

"Of course! At first I didn't even recognize him."

*"Destroyed in the space of a few months. Poor Giancarlo. You can't
know how sorry I am. It's such a trauma. I don't have a dearer friend."*

"You'll see, he won't come in the winter—"

*"Oh, please be quiet! Don't even mention it. And to think of the injustice
of fate. An important man like him, in that condition, and wretched me, who
never did a blessed thing, with my iron constitution."*

*"You're telling me? You know that at my last checkup they found me—
in their words—like a little girl, perfect from head to toe, inside and out . . ."*

Doctor Toro breaks off and with a wave of his hand invites me to continue. I am ready:

*The monsignor is also disturbed by two very excited young men who are wear-
ing strange athletic outfits and trying to attract attention to themselves.*

*"Do you have the enlargement with you?" one asks the other in a loud
voice.*

"I hope so. But you have to dig through this stack of papers to find it."

*He rummages through a leather briefcase, and after a little while, he
draws out a large photograph: it shows a gigantic pear-shaped wall of rock and
ice. The young man points to an area precisely in the center of the photograph.*

*"Here it is. You can't see it in the small print. We will naturally have to
examine it up close, but one could say that this perpendicular ledge is actually
detached from the rockface, and that behind it there is something like a shaft, or
a tunnel. I would swear that you can go through—"*

Doctor Toro bursts out laughing. *"Formidable!* We're in rare form tonight. These seemingly unconnected fragments fit perfectly together
to signify a leitmotiv: the future. The husband and wife, the monsignor, the two women, the two mountain climbers are all thinking of
the time to come, they have a sort of blind faith in it. But now that the
story has developed and found a meaning, we must give these characters a setting. Tell me: where do you prefer that we put them?"

"No," I say, "you won't trap me this time. I may not be very
crafty, but from the very beginning I knew where I was heading. And
I'm amused that you should ask for my assistance. But enough now.
It's as plain as day: the husband and wife, the monsignor, the two
women, and the two mountain climbers are travelling. Where? From

the episode with the married couple we can infer that the destination is South America. How are they going there? On an ocean liner perhaps? But no: if that were the case, the monsignor would be able to solve his problem in the peace and quiet of his own cabin. So how are they travelling? It must be by air! There is no other alternative. And now it will happen, right? The accident, the crash, the sudden catastrophe, the thing from which the conversations and worries we have described, all focused on the future, will acquire a cruel, ironic significance. I didn't expect this from you, dear Doctor Toro. It's much too banal, truly unworthy of you who are usually so imaginative. No, forget about the airplane. Let's start over instead."

The old doctor answers me with one of his malign little smiles.

"It isn't my fault," he exclaims. "I swear, I myself would have been more cautious, but . . ." And he points toward the sky.

I look up. At that moment a plane is emerging from a huge storm cloud that is rapidly passing overhead—the sky is in fact clearing—at an appreciable altitude of not more than three thousand meters. Its right wing is trailing a thin, dense plume of black smoke. Something disastrous has happened, and the plane is losing altitude in search of a possible landing field.

Paralyzed with amazement at the diabolical coincidence, I am silent. Three or four seconds pass, then a black, smoking object breaks away from the plane and, after tracing the briefest curve, plummets with lightning speed.

"My God, that's an engine!"

Doctor Toro nods yes.

The plane, now smoking a little less, proceeds on course without banking, and I am already reassuring myself when it suddenly begins to roll over and over and the wings, like the blades in a fan, describe four, five, eight very rapid circles.

Then, as if it were carrying out a suicide pondered for a long time, the plane points its nose toward the surface of the earth and falls vertically, with all its might (or so it seems).

The gigantic coffin disappears behind the crest of a nearby hill. And that's it. There is no crash or explosion, no flames or smoke.

"It's frightening," I say, breathless. "You're the Devil himself."

He turns to me, pale but calm:

"They were up there."

"Who? The married couple, the monsignor, the ladies, the mountain climbers?"

He nods yes.

"And how did you come to know it?"

"How did *we* come to know it, you mean. You too were a contributor. It's simple: we are the ones who made the plane crash."

"No, there wasn't any disaster in our story. We mentioned only conversations, that's all."

"But the content of the conversations foreshadowed the disaster, in fact rendered it inevitable, from the point of view of the narrative. You yourself recognized it."

"Nonsense! You're mad. And no matter what you say, I had no part in it. The airplane was your idea, right from the start. I had no part in it, I tell you."

"Calm down. Don't take it that way. Even without the air crash it would have been the same for those people."

"What are you saying?"

"Absolutely the same. The future, calculations about what will happen, plans . . . catastrophes. You saw, didn't you, how this thing fell. Do you think the hours, days, months, years that cascade over us move any slower?"

(1971)

A
Difficult
Evening

With a strange urgency my old friend Gianni Soterini invited me to supper at his villa in Bograte, about twenty kilometers outside the city, in the heart of the forest of Slenta. It is a hilly area, snobbish and isolated.

When I arrived a little before eight, I immediately perceived, from the facial expressions and the tone of the voices, that something was not right.

I was welcomed by the beautiful Stefania, Gianni's wife: "I am sorry you have to see me like this. Just last night Aunt Gorgona had one of her usual crises."

Aunt Gorgona, the sister of Gianni's father, is a corpulent person, rather eccentric and moody.

"What kind of crisis?" I asked, deliberately tactless.

Stefania tried to gloss over the incident: "But all she needs is a pill. Now she's sleeping like a baby."

In the meantime, Aunt Gorgona had appeared at the top of the staircase, irreproachable, wearing a long black dress, her shoulders wrapped in a shawl that was popular fifty years ago. And she was covered with all her diamonds.

She came to greet me, smiling. "What a pleasure, dear." She took my arm and pulled me toward the door that leads to the garden, insensible to the calls ("Aunt, please!").

"They probably told you that I was off my rocker, right?" she whispered as soon as we were alone. "That I had one of my crises. It's true, I can't deny it. Such childish things. Of course, there will always be crises. But to be afraid. . . . You noticed it, I imagine."

"Afraid of what?"

"Paolomaria and Foffino . . . yes, the boys, the children. . . . There was a phone call that said they were coming here tonight with a group of their friends."

"A call from whom?"

"Anonymous, of course."

"But even if they arrive—"

"The call added that the little ones were coming to do away with papa and mama—" and here she burst into a hearty laugh.

Stefania was calling us. "Please, come to the table. What were you two plotting?"

We were joined at the table by old Father Emigera, the family's confessor for three generations. He and I were the only guests.

"I imagine," Gianni began, "that Aunt Gorgona has already explained everything to you."

"I don't know if she told me 'everything,' but—"

"So what do you think of it?" Stefania intervened.

"An anonymous phone call . . ."—this was certain to gain time—"maybe it's a stupid joke."

Gianni was serious: "I don't think so. In the months before they went away to college, Paolomaria used to look at us in a certain way."

"Foffino too, for that matter," said Stefania.

"But why don't you just lock the doors and windows?"

"That's the worst thing we could do," said Gianni. "It would aggravate them even more."

"But college will keep them in line, won't it?"

"Don't make me laugh. Paolomaria is such a devil. . . . He could escape from Alcatraz."

"Would Paolomaria and Foffino really come to kill you?"

He shook his head as if to say: it is inevitable.

And Stefania: "This is the way things are today. Parents are killed today. It's the latest fad."

"Killed? Who was killed?" It was the troubled voice of Father Emigera, in the clouds as usual.

"Us, Gianni and me!" Stefania snapped, exasperated. "The children are coming to do away with us—understand, Father? To do away with Gianni and me, Gianni and me—"

"Calm down, Stefania," Aunt Gorgona interrupted. "Please don't make a scene. . . . After all, let's be honest, these kids are not entirely wrong."

"What do you mean?"

"It isn't that they're all wrong. Let's be fair. What kind of life can they look forward to? What kind of example have we set for them? What have we done to guarantee them a happy future? If they protest, contest, revolt, how can we blame them?"

"But in this case they actually want to kill us," Gianni dared to object.

"Kill, kill! What a pessimist you are!" Aunt Gorgona was in rare form. "While we're waiting, let's consider how they'll go about it. It wasn't said that they would be so wicked. It wasn't said that they would cut you into little pieces. It wasn't said that they would douse you with gasoline and burn you alive. I may understand Paolomaria better than you. He has such a big heart. Paolomaria is a generous boy. . . . I would swear that he won't make you suffer."

"What?"

"I don't know, maybe it will be a shot in the neck. . . . Or zip— a blade in the cardiac muscle. . . . Ah, that would be beautiful!" Aunt Gorgona shook with laughter.

Gianni turned pale. He changed his mind. He called the butler Ernesto. "Listen, Ernesto, don't worry about us. Please hurry and close the doors and windows. And make sure they're locked."

"Locked?" said Father Emigera. "Why are you closing them? It's hot tonight, really, Stefania, aren't you hot?"

"Yes, it's hot, Father," Aunt Gorgona chimed in. "But in this case they're shutting up everything because they're afraid that the brood is returning to the nest to get rid of the parents."

Until this point I had been only an observer. "If you are so afraid, why do you stay here? You should flee, shouldn't you? The world is a big place. Your dear children won't follow you to the North Pole!"

Gianni: "Flee? Where? This is my home, this is my family's old house. Flee where? No, no, I prefer to confront my fate."

"Fate!" It was Aunt Gorgona again. "What a big word. . . . They are your sons, after all. . . . And I understand them, the poor boys. . . . You gave them life, and they are coming to take it away from you. . . . The account will be settled in a certain sense, right?"

Stefania: "What do you want me to tell you? Think whatever you like, you can think I'm senile, but I find the whole thing a little exaggerated."

"Did you hear that?" said Gianni, lowering his voice.

"What?"

"Those steps on the gravel. . . . Did you hear them?"

"I didn't," said Stefania.

Father Emigera looked at the clock (coffee was now being served). "I'm sorry, my friends, but tonight at the church . . . the culture committee is meeting again. . . . I wouldn't want to be discourteous."

He stood up, brushing the bread crumbs from his cassock with his right hand.

I too stood up.

"No, not you, Buzzati," Stefania protested, pleading. "It's still early. You have to try some of this tart. Another tiny half hour, please. . . . Shall we go and sit over there by the fireplace?"

Aunt Gorgona: "Let him go, Stefania. The prospect of being a witness isn't very attractive. . . . Forgive me, but I couldn't bear"— she was unable to repress her giggles—"to witness your execution."

There was a moment of silence. And in that silence the night entered, the mysterious rustling of the garden, of the country, the trees, branches, leaves, meadow, the animals' faint voices, the wolves' soft padding through the paths, the wild rabbits, the elves, the crickets' lament, the liquid hiss of the snails and the snakes, the impalpable grating of the grasshoppers and spiders. And amid all these nocturnal sounds, forcing them to strain their ears, was a distant tread over the grass and twigs, very soft, scarcely audible.

"Did you hear that?" Gianni repeated, pale as death.

"No, Gianni, I didn't hear anything."

Coward that I am, I stood up again.

"It's late, Gianni. Forgive me, but tomorrow morning I must leave for Trieste at 7:30. Anyhow it seems clear that it was all some sort of bad joke."

Aunt Gorgona practically jumped out of her chair. "Of course! A joke! How is it possible that you, Gianni and Stefania, still haven't gotten it?"

It was Aunt Gorgona who wanted to accompany me to the door. (Gianni and Stefania were too exhausted to move from the table.) And she told me: "They will be here in a little while, I can feel it. But they aren't bad boys, believe me, my dear friend, they will take care of everything with the smallest expense of energy, without a fuss . . . and painlessly. . . . It won't take but a few seconds, you'll see, what I have in mind is that little shot in the neck."

I had already started the engine of my car. I rolled down the window.

"But you, Aunt Gorgona . . . I wouldn't want you to get involved too."

She burst into another hearty laugh: "Me? Of course I will be involved. In fact, from the beginning . . . Do you want me to abandon my nephews? . . . Besides, I have known them for many, many years. . . . We've worked so hard, haven't we? splendidly, patiently we have fixed things so this might happen, can you deny it? (I shook my head no.) . . . But go on, hurry, my dear, so you can avoid the trouble. . . . I sense a certain suspicious movement over there, among the bushes."

She turned toward the pitch darkness and asked, affectionately: "Paolomaria . . . Foffino . . . Are you here?"

(1971)

Kafka's Houses

During a trip to Prague I grew curious to see the places associated with Franz Kafka.

From the very beginning of my writing career, Kafka has been my cross. I have not written a story, novel, or play in which someone has not perceived resemblances, derivations, imitations, or simply shameless plagiarisms at the Czech writer's expense. Several critics proclaimed guilty analogies even when I dispatched a telegram to the contrary or offered a detailed list of differences between our writing.

All of this has determined my attitude toward Kafka for many years: I have suffered not from an inferiority complex, but from an annoyance complex. The result has been that I have lost any desire to read his work, as well as biographies and essays that deal with him. Given this situation, however, it would have been a mean affront if I had not sought out his spirit here in Prague. Nonetheless, my dear friends will say that I was compelled precisely by that attraction that induces the criminal to return to the scene of the crime.

Of course I would have preferred to make this pilgrimage incognito. But I still needed a guide. Who could help me? One night at Tatranská Lomnica in the High Tatras, I met a gentleman named Emil Kacirek. He was a very well-educated person, a polyglot with a singularly penetrating mind who worked at an international advertising firm in Prague. In addition to Czech, French, German, Spanish, English, Russian, Polish, Hungarian, Slovenian, and Hindi, he knew Italian quite well and had read one of my books. At one time he too had been a writer, serving as literary critic for a review, among other things. Then he chose to stop and cited the example of Rimbaud.

Since he knew who I was, we got along well together, and with affectionate insistence, he made me swear that I would contact him if I ever passed through Prague. No matter what he was busy with, he would leave work to show me the city. I did not then make any particular requests, but it was clear that if anyone existed who knew everything there was to know about Kafka, it had to be Emil Kacirek. And there could be no doubt that he was in the dark concerning the controversy between Kafka and me.

I arrived in Prague late at night. The next morning I telephoned the number that Kacirek had given me.

"Just a minute, please," answered a woman.

I heard confused voices, doors closing, typewriters ticking away. Then a different voice got on the line; it was another woman.

"Emil Kacirek? Hold on; I will call him for you."

There was the sound of steps drawing away, and I heard a click, which probably meant that the call was being transferred. Finally, a man spoke: "Emil Kacirek will be in around ten o'clock."

I called back at 10:10. Again there was a female voice: "Just a minute, please." Then a pause, steps drawing away, the click from the switchboard, silence. It seemed that the call had been cut off before someone on the other end had been able to transfer it. (I later learned that the people of Prague had had to get used to these mysterious telephone interruptions.)

I tried two more times with the same result. Then I took a taxi and located the address printed on Kacirek's card. It was the Chamber of Commerce. I entered the building; on the left stood a wood-and-glass booth that housed two elderly telephone operators.

"Emil Kacirek, please."

"Just a minute, please," said the oldest one, and after she dialed the number, she muttered something in Czech. Then she immediately informed me: "He is waiting for you in the lobby of the Palace Hotel."

And they tell me that I imitate Kafka. It's life, I would say. Neither on the telephone nor at the Chamber of Commerce had I said who I was. And I had spoken German, with much difficulty to be sure, but it was still German. How, then, did Kacirek learn that I had arrived in Prague and was looking for him? Did he perhaps belong to a sinister organization that followed the slightest move of every foreigner who visited Czechoslovakia? Or was he simply a sorcerer?

All the same, the episode was propitious. If the latter possibility were in fact the case, at the very least Kacirek might procure me an interview with the legendary Golem. As for Kafka, it would be enough for me to make the briefest allusion, without compromising myself, and Kacirek would probably bury me beneath an avalanche of unheard-of information.

The message I had been given was precise. Kacirek was waiting for me in the lobby of the Palace Hotel. Yet he seemed depressed. It unfortunately turned out that as the only person in Prague who knew Hindi, he had been officially assigned to accompany a small group of important Indian tourists to Marienbad.

"What a shame," he said. "You can't imagine how sorry I am. . . . And to think that I had prepared a special itinerary just for you . . . the places where Kafka lived, you know, his houses and haunts and so forth. You would have found it interesting, dear Buzzati, wouldn't you?"

I did not answer. I said good-bye, thanking him. Then I took a taxi to the Italian Consulate in Malá Strana. There I would certainly find some helpful information. Within the space of ten minutes, in fact, the amiable ambassador introduced me to Professor Domenico

Caccamo, Director of the Italian Cultural Institute. He was certainly the most well-qualified person for what I wanted.

A specialist in Polish, Czech, and Hungarian history, Professor Caccamo was a very cordial and animated young man. He seemed delighted to act as my guide. He had just a few free hours and could take me in his car to see the most beautiful things.

I could not have hoped for more pleasant company. But I think that I would have preferred someone less informed about Italian literature. Because of that annoyance complex I mentioned earlier, I did not say a word about Kafka to him. Should the condemned be the first to speak of the rope?

But then, as we were about to arrive at the Old Town Square, Caccamo stopped the car in front of the Church of St. Nicholas.

"I don't know whether you might be interested in this," he said, pointing to a dignified gray building, "but Kafka was born in that house, on the first floor."

He was not smiling. There was not a trace of irony in his voice. I was silent. It is a three-floor house in the baroque style, crowned with elaborate dormer windows. It stands on the corner between Kaprova and Maislova Streets and bears the number 5. I felt cold, but it was a sunny day.

My unforgettable trek through one of the most fantastic cities in the world lasted more than four hours. But every so often Caccamo said, "By the way," then stopped the car, lowered his window, and held out his hand. "They say that Kafka lived in that house, if you are at all interested."

He did the same near the Týn Church, on Tynska Street, where there is an old, very pretty little house at No. 7. He did the same near the city hall, where there is an ancient apartment building covered with graffiti on mythological themes. "They say that Kafka lived in that house." He did the same in the Bilekstrasse, in the Lagenasse, in the incredible Golden or Alchemists' Lane, behind the cathedral, which is lined with toy houses two or three meters tall that look as if they had sprung from a child's dream. He did the same in the street that runs down Strachov Hill and in a number of other streets, lanes, and alleys that I did not have time to note. "They say that . . ." And he did not smile. "If you are at all interested. . . ." And there wasn't the slightest trace of irony in his voice.

At a certain point, I asked: "But what is it with this Kafka? Did he have the gift of ubiquity? Is it possible that in forty years he could have lived in so many houses?"

Caccamo answered: "The fact is that Kafka was discovered here just two years ago. Before that no one knew that he existed. Then there was a Kafkamania. Today there are hundreds of houses where Kafka is alleged to have lived, just as in northern Italy there are so many beds in which Napoleon slept."

Was he joking? Was he elegantly pulling my leg? Was he ironizing on the Kafkaesque evil eye that dogged me? Was he speaking seriously, or had all those stops been signs of his mordant wit?

The next morning, before departing, I hurried to find a professional tour guide, a native of Prague who could not know anything at all about me. I came across Jirina Klenkova, the pretty thirty-year-old wife of a lawyer. She spoke a halting but precise Italian. In a word, she was most competent.

"What would you like to see?" she asked.

"Kafka," I said, exasperated. I could speak frankly with her. "Everything that has to do with Kafka."

And with marvelous precision Jirina Klenkova took me to see where Kafka was born, where Kafka studied, where Kafka spent his adolescence, where Kafka usually took his walks, where Kafka worked as an employee of an insurance company, where Kafka retired to meditate and write, where Kafka did this, where Kafka did that: I lost count of all the houses, but they corresponded exactly to those that Caccamo had shown me. Evidently, he was quite familiar with them and had pretended to be joking, but joke he did not.

The only difference was that in the end Jirina Klenkova proposed something that Professor Caccamo may have thought of proposing but perhaps had not explicitly done so to avoid displeasing me. "Would you like to see his grave?" she asked. His last house.

The gate of the Old Jewish Cemetery was wide open at eleven o'clock in the morning. There was a high wall around the perimeter, a slight chill in the air, silence, and not a living soul. The many rows of graves, all marked with upright stones, extended as far as the eye could see.

"Over here," said Signora Klenkova, walking toward the right along the path between the perimeter wall and the first row of graves. The dry snow creaked beneath our feet. I read name after name of people who no longer existed: Kornfeld, Pollak, Stein, Rosenberg, Loewit, Strauss, Freud, Weiss, Goldsmith, Loewy, Rosenbaum, and so on. Not a living soul. The hungry sparrows chirped here and there. It was a day of pale sunlight; I remember it well.

Kafka's grave is different from the others. Instead of a granite slab, there is a hexagonal marker tapered at the top. It is made of gray stone, pitted like travertine. I felt cold. The first name reads: "Dr. Franz Kafka, 1883–1924." Below is the father: "Hermann Kafka, 1854–1931." Then the mother: "Julie Kafka, 1856–1934."

A small square of space is roped off in front of the marker. In this space I saw a broken glass vase thrust into the earth at an angle, three old flowers that had apparently withered, and several fir branches concealed by the snow, the last of the winter. There was an immense silence. And solitude. The border of the grave is lined with many small stones. "It is the Jews' homage to their dead," explained Signora Klenkova. "They place them two by two. It commemorates the ancient desert. Moses. The dead were buried in the sand, and some stones were placed on top of the grave. To indicate that there was a body underneath."

Behind the grave a row of tall black stones turned their backs to us. I went to have a look at them. "Wilhelm Kafka, officer, 1862–1932." "Julie Kafkova, 1860–1938." "Rudolph Herz, Eduard Herz." "Karolina Margoliusova, Salomoun Margolius."

"Excuse me, sir," said Signora Klenkova. "Are you writing a study of Kafka? No Italian tourist has ever asked me for information about Kafka. You are the first. Are you studying him?"

"No," I answered, and explained everything to her.

The kind Signora Klenkova shook her head, expressing her sympathy. She smiled with the proper melancholy. "I understand," she said. With her right hand, she gestured at Kafka, who slept below, and again she smiled slightly. "But it isn't his fault, is it?"

A fat raven perched on top of the stone of Yehuda Goldstern, 1896–1941. And then he began to run his beak slowly through his feathers.

(1965)

Design by David Bullen
Typeset in Mergenthaler Bembo
with Helvetica display
by Wilsted & Taylor
Printed by Maple-Vail
on acid-free paper